WELCOME

Few artists are truly deserving of the title 'legend', but Sir Paul McCartney is one such person. A gifted musician, masterful songwriter, creative composer and passionate campaigner – with a career spanning more than six decades, the significance of McCartney's enduring impact is cemented in music history. Now, nearly 60 years after the rise of Beatlemania, Macca is still going strong, his songs as resonant and popular as ever.

This book celebrates McCartney's life and work, from The Beatles' heyday, through to his continued success with Wings and impressive solo career, as well as his astonishing musicianship, wide-ranging influence and unmatched legacy. With such a vast and prestigious back-catalogue, many musicians would be content to rest on their laurels – but not Macca. The past few years have seen the release of his latest critically acclaimed studio album, *McCartney III*; the documentary series *The Beatles: Get Back* and his highly anticipated book, *The Lyrics: 1956 to the Present*. If that weren't enough to keep him busy, McCartney returned to the Glastonbury Festival in 2022 for a phenomenal headline set.

It's clear Sir Paul still has plenty of stories to tell and songs to sing, and we can't wait to discover what he'll do next. Macca, we salute you!

Getty

THE STORY OF
PAUL McCARTNEY

Future PLC Quay House, The Ambury, Bath, BA1 1UA

Editorial
Author **Joel McIver**
Editor **Jacqueline Snowden**
Senior Designer **Phil Martin**
Senior Art Editor **Andy Downes**
Head of Art & Design **Greg Whitaker**
Editorial Director **Jon White**

Contributors
Tony Bacon, Briony Duguid, Newton Ribeiro De Oliveira, Jon Wells

Cover images
Press material via DawBell; Getty Images

Photography
All copyrights and trademarks are recognised and respected

Advertising
Media packs are available on request
Commercial Director **Clare Dove**

International
Head of Print Licensing **Rachel Shaw**
licensing@futurenet.com
www.futurecontenthub.com

Circulation
Head of Newstrade **Tim Mathers**

Production
Head of Production **Mark Constance**
Production Project Manager **Matthew Eglinton**
Advertising Production Manager **Joanne Crosby**
Digital Editions Controller **Jason Hudson**
Production Managers **Keely Miller, Nola Cokely,
Vivienne Calvert, Fran Twentyman**

Printed in the UK

Distributed by Marketforce, 5 Churchill Place, Canary Wharf, London, E14 5HU
www.marketforce.co.uk Tel: 0203 787 9001

The Story of Paul McCartney Second Edition (MUB4935)
© 2022 Future Publishing Limited

Future plc is a public
company quoted on the
London Stock Exchange
(symbol: FUTR)
www.futureplc.com

Chief executive **Zillah Byng-Thorne**
Non-executive chairman **Richard Huntingford**
Chief financial officer **Penny Ladkin-Brand**

Tel +44 (0)1225 442 244

Contents

Chapter 1
EARLY DAYS

A young George, John and Paul standing outside Paul's family home where they often rehearsed, circa 1960.

MOTHER NATURE'S SON

How did a kid from suburban Merseyside become the world's greatest songwriter? From Sir Paul's birth to the beginning of The Beatles, here's how it happened

Words: Joel McIver. Image: Getty

Even a rock star knight of the realm has to start somewhere, and for James Paul McCartney – as no-one ever calls him – that somewhere was Walton in Liverpool, where he was born on 18 June 1942. His mother Mary was a midwife, his father Jim was a jazz musician, and he had a younger brother, Michael and later, a stepsister, Ruth.

A clever kid, McCartney was one of only three students at his primary school to pass the 11-plus exam in 1953, enabling him to attend the Liverpool Institute, a grammar school. He met George Harrison there in '54, and the two became friends despite the year's difference in their ages, a big deal to any teenager.

Life might have proceeded along relatively standard lines for him from this point, had fate not intervened. Tragically, Mary died in 1956 after complications from breast cancer surgery. Aged just 14 at the time, McCartney carried the pain of that loss for the rest of his life; it's equally sad to consider that Mary never got to see her son become the most successful musician in the world. Life can be cruel, as none other than John Lennon would have agreed; he lost his own mother when he was 17, a shared experience which led him and McCartney to bond in later years.

A more positive development in the young McCartney's life came about when he became interested in, and then obsessed with, rock and roll music. Liverpool, then the logical source for

imported American records as it was a destination for transatlantic freight, was perhaps the best possible place to be in the late Fifties for a kid into loud music. McCartney had already taken piano lessons and sung in his local church choir, and needed no encouragement to take up the guitar, trading in a trumpet which Jim had given him as a birthday present for a Framus acoustic. He immediately began to write rock and roll songs, his first being 'I Lost My Little Girl', and performed Little Richard's 'Long Tall Sally' at a Butlins holiday camp in Filey.

And so his path was set – helped along, perhaps unexpectedly, by the return of a form of music that was long out of fashion. Skiffle, dead in the water for a decade or more in its home country of the United States, had seized British schoolkids' imaginations for two reasons – it was loud enough to irritate their Frank Sinatra-adoring parents, and you could make the instruments yourself, an important consideration in those barely post-war days.

A skiffle band, The Quarrymen, had formed in November 1956, based around John Lennon, at 16 a year older than McCartney. They rehearsed at his aunt's house or at the family home of the other guitar player, Eric Griffiths. Other musicians came and went but a relatively stable line-up soon coalesced with 'tea chest' bassist Len Garry, washboard player Pete Shotton, drummer Colin Hanton and banjo player Rod Davis. An early member, Nigel Walley, became the group's

designated manager, and secured local gigs while the band built a setlist of cover songs, including Gene Vincent's 'Be-Bop-a-Lula' and the biggest skiffle hit of all, 'Rock Island Line' by "King of Skiffle", Lonnie Donegan.

The Quarrymen were making relatively decent progress by the summer of '57, having come second in a Liverpool talent contest and played a show at the soon-to-be-legendary Cavern Club. On 6 July, the group played at the St Peter's Church Rose Queen garden fête in Woolton. This auspicious gig took place on the back of a moving flatbed lorry as part of a procession of floats containing Guides, Scouts, Cubs and other youth groups. The main act was a display by a pack of police dogs... we said that even the greatest of us have to start somewhere, right?

McCartney attended the gig, and was introduced to Lennon after The Quarrymen's set by a former bassist with the band, Ivan Vaughan. The two musicians talked while the group set up for a second performance, this time at an evening dance in the church hall. McCartney played a few songs for Lennon, who was impressed enough with the youngster to suggest – via Pete Shotton – that he should join the band. When Shotton mentioned this to McCartney two weeks later, he accepted the invitation, on condition that he could go to Scout camp in Derbyshire and then a family holiday at Butlins first.

By the time McCartney joined the band, Shotton and Davis had quit The Quarrymen. The

A six-year-old Paul with his older brother Mike, pictured in 1948.

Paul performing at Liverpool's Cavern Club, circa 1960, when The Beatles were starting out.

new line-up of Lennon, McCartney, Griffiths, Garry and Hanton rehearsed strenuously – by schoolboy standards, at least – and played their first of a run of shows on 18 October that year. Songs included the Everly Brothers' 'Bye Bye Love' and Elvis Presley's 'All Shook Up', and as time passed the setlist moved away from skiffle and towards rock and roll. Buddy Holly and the Crickets were an influence when it came to original songs, two of which included Lennon's 'Hello Little Girl' and McCartney's 'I Lost My Little Girl', which shared an obvious common theme.

The strands of history were coming together at this point, with George Harrison – then only 14 – auditioning as a Quarryman in March 1958 with a rendition of 'Guitar Boogie Shuffle'. It's thought that Lennon regarded his future guitar partner to be too young for membership, but McCartney pushed for Harrison's recruitment; the senior musician eventually relented. Another friend of McCartney's, pianist John Duff Lowe, then joined The Quarrymen, which now had an unusual four-guitarist line-up – the three future superstars plus Eric Griffiths. Some political manoeuvring ensued, with Lennon and

Getty

Mike and Jim McCartney surrounded by Paul's fan mail at the Forthlin Road family home.

An early lineup of The Beatles performing at the Top Ten Club in Hamburg, Germany in 1961. Left to right: Pete Best (background), Paul McCartney (on piano), George Harrison, John Lennon and Stuart Sutcliffe.

"If you can play your stuff in a pub, then you're a good band."

Paul McCartney

McCartney keen for Griffiths to switch to bass; when he refused, they persuaded manager Walley to fire him. Walley himself departed soon after, and Len Garry contracted tubercular meningitis, quitting the band out of necessity.

With the band reasonably stable once again, it was decided that it was time to record some songs. A session was booked for 12 July 1958 at Phillips' Sound Recording Services in Liverpool, and two songs – a McCartney/Harrison original called 'In Spite of All the Danger' and a cover of Buddy Holly's 'That'll Be the Day' – were recorded direct to vinyl via a single microphone. The disc, now valued as the most expensive bit of wax ever manufactured, is in McCartney's hands to this day; fortunately you can hear the recordings on YouTube, where the voice of the young Lennon – who sang both songs – sounds startlingly proficient.

Still, 1958 was not to be the best year of The Quarrymen's short but promising career. Hanton and Lowe quit the band; Lennon's mother Julia

was killed in a car accident in July, leaving him distraught; and McCartney and Harrison played with a Welsh skiffle group called The Vikings. Gigs were few and far between, and the group changed its name to Johnny & The Moondogs and then to the bizarre Japage 3, a combination of letters from their names. In the end it was Harrison who saved the day, inviting guitarist Ken Brown and drummer Pete Best from the Les Stewart Quartet – with whom he had played in a hiatus from the practically defunct Quarrymen – to join him, Lennon and McCartney, in a 'new' Quarrymen in 1959.

By early 1960, Brown had been replaced by Lennon's art-school chum Stuart Sutcliffe, who took up the bass guitar. A recording, 'One After 909', was attempted, as was a rehearsal tape, but by now the band were sick of The Quarrymen name: it was clear that a new identity was needed.

After some thought, Lennon and Sutcliffe came up with an entirely brand-new band name. You'll never guess what it was. ⬇

Paul's stepsister, Ruth, and stepmother, Angela, pictured with Jim McCartney outside the house – Rembrandt – in Heswall that Paul bought for his father.

Starting out

Paul (centre) with George (left, facing away) and John (right) performing at Liverpool's Cavern Club, in August 1962.

BEAT THIS

Some bands are big. Some bands are huge – but The Beatles were the biggest thing that's ever happened to popular music. Here's how Paul McCartney and the Fab Four took over the world

The story of The Beatles, the biggest pop or rock band there has ever been or will ever be, has multiple strands – but for our purposes, the most relevant strand is how the group's babyfaced bassist gradually took control of it, revealing himself as a songwriter, lyricist and visionary without equal in doing so.

The Beatles – whose name was based on a pun, 'beat' being a fashionable name for rock music – were only a functioning band for around a decade, excluding the brief 'Threetles' comeback in the Nineties. In that time, though, they redefined the entire concept of popular music, kickstarting at least three musical genres – psychedelia, progressive rock and heavy metal – and reaping financial rewards unlike those of any other musical entity in history, Elvis Presley being the only arguable exception.

The Fab Four at the photoshoot for the *Twist and Shout* EP cover, in April 1963.

Words: Joel McIver. Image: Getty

Of course, in the space available here we can only give an impression of the quartet's immense cultural impact, but we can certainly celebrate the many high points of their career, with the obvious focus being on the work of Paul McCartney. What's most interesting from our perspective is that he started his life in the band very much as the junior partner to the older, more experienced and more aggressive John Lennon. The Quarrymen had effectively been Lennon's band; he had taken almost all the vocals; he had lent his name to their brief incarnation as Johnny & The Moondogs; and he even assigned the most boring instrument in any band, the bass guitar, to McCartney, once Stuart Sutcliffe had left the band in 1961. The Beatles were, at this stage, very much 'Lennon plus supporting musicians' – McCartney, George Harrison and Pete Best.

Much of The Beatles' time in 1960 and '61 was spent playing a relentless series of gigs, many of them several hours in length, at Liverpool's Cavern Club and at the Star-Club in Hamburg, Germany. They played over 300 shows at the former venue, a veritable sweatbox of a club where they evolved from gauche youngsters into a rock and roll band of considerable power.

Future David Bowie drummer Mick 'Woody' Woodmansey once visited the Cavern, and observed: "It was sweaty, and packed out. There were shelves all down one side of a curved wall, and I noticed that as the night went on, pint glasses were stacking up there. Some of them were full, or nearly full, and I remember thinking that was weird, because people apparently weren't drinking their beer. But then I realised that you couldn't get out of the club, so if you needed to urinate, you had to piss in the pint glasses and then put them on the shelves. The place stank as a result."

As for the Star-Club, this was where the boys began to make steps towards being men. Drugs were an everyday part of the Hamburg experience, at least by the standards of 60 years ago: The Beatles regularly used Preludin, a form of amphetamine, to keep their energy levels up over the long, exhausting gigs. A further challenge for McCartney, assigned the role of bass player, was to sing and play his parts at the same time.

"The danger with bass is that everybody else has got the interesting jobs and you're just the last guy to get a part, and literally you get the root notes, two in a bar," he told the writer Tony Bacon in 1994 (read the full interview on page 58). "From the word go, once I got over the fact that I was lumbered with the bass, I did get quite proud to be a bass player, quite proud of the idea. Once you realised the control you had over the band, you were in control."

Later in his career McCartney became deservedly famous for the spiralling, counterpointed basslines which he played, but that's not to say that the parts weren't also challenging in the early years of the band. Take 'I

Pete Best, John, Paul and George posing with vials of the energy-boosting drug Preludin while at The Star Club in Hamburg, May 1962.

"This teen-friendly, eager-to-please opening stage of The Beatles' career soon matured into a deeper, more thoughtful approach, both musically and philosophically – and especially so in the case of McCartney."

Saw Her Standing There', for instance, which has a fast-moving bass-line that cuts across the vocal part, making it doubly difficult to execute.

"Because some of these parts were independent melodic parts, it became much more difficult to sing, it was like doing this [pats his head and rubs his stomach]," he told Bacon. "So I had to put a little special effort into that, which made it very interesting."

Things moved quickly for The Beatles from that point on. A recording for the singer Tony Sheridan on his version of 'My Bonnie', on which they were credited as the Beat Brothers, led them to a meeting with Brian Epstein, whose family owned a record shop in Liverpool called NEMS. A crucial figure in the band's progression, Epstein became their manager in early 1962, was responsible for telling Pete Best in August that he

was being replaced by sometime Rory Storm drummer Ringo Starr, and arranged auditions with record labels in London. In October '62 a debut single, 'Love Me Do', was released by the Parlophone label – and, as we now know, The Beatles were set for stardom.

At this point the Fab Four, as they were soon to be known, could have followed the same path as a hundred other Merseybeat acts, enjoying a couple of hits and then a lifetime on the nostalgia circuit – but instead, an entire nation fell for them, hook, line and sinker. An unprecedented sequence of hits followed in 1963, the year of 'Beatlemania'; 'Please Please Me', 'From Me to You', 'She Loves You' and 'I Want to Hold Your Hand' among them. Perhaps Britain was ready for a new sensation; maybe the rise of the teenager, a relatively new demographic, coincided with The

Beatles' arrival – but most of all, the songs' upbeat tempos, catchy vocal harmonies and sleek productions made them inescapable. It also didn't hurt that the main songwriters, Lennon and McCartney, were singing about love, or at least sex disguised as love (see 'Please Please Me').

This teen-friendly, eager-to-please opening stage of The Beatles' career soon matured into a deeper, more thoughtful approach, both musically and philosophically – and especially so in the case of McCartney. Jump forward to 1965 – an astounding five albums into their career – and the world was presented with his first absolute tour de force when it came to songwriting. This was 'Yesterday', a song on the *Help!* album and, depending on the source you consult, the subject of over 2,000 later cover versions. A ballad with a heartbreaking strings

Partners in rhyme: Lennon and McCartney in November 1963.

Getty

Mr tambourine man: the group pose with toy instruments for a portrait in 1964.

Taking a break on the set of the movie *Help!* in 1965.

Performing to over 55,000 screaming fans at Shea Stadium, New York, in August 1965 – the largest concert The Beatles ever played.

backing, the song is deceptively simple but utterly masterful in its melodic choices. Like all great songs, it retains a certain unresolved mystique; arguments still rage to this day about whether McCartney sings "Yesterday came suddenly" or "Yes, today came suddenly".

The same year's *Rubber Soul* album took another step up, this time expanding the musical palette and moving into more obscure, even esoteric lyrical territory. McCartney said of this LP, "We'd had our cute period, and now it was time to expand" – and while this resulted in a whole list of classic songs, it saw the beginnings of tension between him and Lennon, as the younger musician began to flex his creative muscles. The results included 'You Won't See Me', 'Looking Through You' and the bilingual ballad 'Michelle', although it should be noted that McCartney's compositional genius was matched by that of Lennon, whose 'Norwegian Wood', 'Nowhere Man', 'Girl' and 'In My Life' are gold-standard masterpieces.

It has been said that the competitive tension between these two huge talents was what made The Beatles such huge achievers, and there's definitely something to this theory. Other Beatles experts – and there have been many of them over the years – have suggested that a third such talent would have been too much for the band to bear, making it fortunate that Harrison and Starr were

With constant travel and live performances taking their toll, The Beatles stopped touring at the end of August 1966 and continued as a studio band.

content to play a lesser role. Yet another Beatles theory states that McCartney wrote the softer love songs and Lennon the hard rockers, although this is only partly true.

By 1966, McCartney had discovered cannabis and LSD, as had the rest of his band. This goes some way to explaining the artistic direction of the albums released during The Beatles' final golden period until their dissolution four years later. *Revolver* (1966), *Sgt Pepper's Lonely Hearts Club Band* ('67), *The Beatles* (aka *The White Album*, '68) and *Abbey Road* ('69) are the archetypal albums that set the standard for decades to come; the lesser – but still epoch-shaping – LPs *Magical Mystery Tour* ('67), *Yellow Submarine* ('69) and the final, flawed effort *Let It Be* (1970) still bear all the hallmarks of McCartney's prodigious talent.

Revolver is more or less unsurpassed in the musical catalogue of the self-aware Sixties, and contains McCartney-penned gems in the form of 'Paperback Writer', a speedy, bass-driven workout; the still-unmatched 'Eleanor Rigby', on which he was accompanied only by a string ensemble; and the heavenly 'Here, There and Everywhere', a paean to expanded consciousness. He went still further, entering vaudeville territory with 'Good Day Sunshine', writing the perennial primary-school anthem 'Yellow Submarine', adding the Motown-inspired 'Got to Get You into My Life', and composing perhaps the most heart-wrenching breakup song ever written, 'For No One'. Was the man unstoppable?

He may not have been, but The Beatles as a touring unit certainly were, ceasing to play live concert tours in 1966. The live technology of the day was insufficient, we now know, but the music

> **"After Brian died... Paul took over and supposedly led us... That was the disintegration. I thought, 'We've fuckin' had it.'"**
>
> ———
>
> John Lennon,
> *Rolling Stone*,
> 1970

Beatlemania: police officers struggle to hold back the crowd of fans outside Buckingham Palace while The Beatles receive their MBEs, October 1965.

which they were now writing was hardly conducive to the stage in any case. Free to focus on the next step, McCartney did his first outside work, composing some themes for a film score, *The Family Way*. The project bagged him an Ivor Novello Award for Best Instrumental Theme.

A new album, *Sgt Pepper's Lonely Hearts Club Band*, appeared in 1967 and is inextricably tied in with that year's Summer of Love, when the hippie movement peaked and when it genuinely seemed that worldwide love and unity would heal ongoing social ills such as the Vietnam War, then into its eighth year. The LP was utterly surreal, musically and artistically, with McCartney's concept of a travelling circus removing all boundaries from the group's creativity.

Harrison recorded the sitar-heavy 'Within You Without You'; Starr stepped up to the mic for 'With a Little Help from My Friends'; both Lennon and McCartney revisited old music-hall sounds for 'Being for the Benefit of Mr Kite!' and 'When I'm Sixty Four'; and the world seemed to end in apocalyptic fashion with the colossal album-closer 'A Day in the Life'. Mostly written by Lennon but with its high point a mesmeric midsection composed by McCartney, the song

Paul with manager Brian Epstein (left) on the set of *Top of the Pops* in June 1966. Epstein's death in August 1967 seemed to mark the beginning of the end for The Beatles.

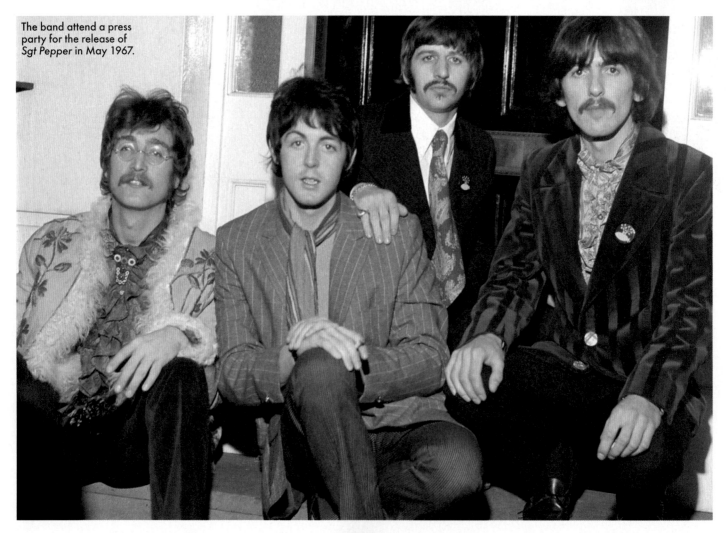

The band attend a press party for the release of *Sgt Pepper* in May 1967.

Relaxing in London: Paul plays while John sunbathes in the background, summer 1967.

Thumbs up: McCartney during the production of feature-length cartoon *Yellow Submarine*, in February 1968.

moves inexorably to a terrifying, full-orchestra climax – and the nonsensical 'infinite groove' which ends the LP.

Amid his other achievements with this and other Beatles albums, McCartney's command of the bass guitar seems almost trivial – but those inventive *Sgt Pepper* lines made him an icon among bass players. "I started to realise the power you had within the band," he told Tony Bacon. "Even though the whole band is going in A you could go in E, and they'd go 'let us off the hook!' You're actually in control then, an amazing thing. So I sussed that and got particularly interested in playing the bass. And then I took it beyond that. I thought well, if you can do that, what else can you do? You might even be able to play notes that aren't in the chord. I just started to experiment: what could you do? Well, maybe you can use different notes. Sevenths instead of the regular notes, or maybe even a little tune through the chords that doesn't exist anywhere else. That idea of an independent melody."

Now was McCartney's moment to step forward and assume greater control of the band – enabled, to an extent, by the tragic suicide of Brian Epstein

in August 1967. His first idea was to suggest a Beatles movie, which later became *Magical Mystery Tour*. McCartney directed most of the film, although the accompanying soundtrack album did better; two years later, the animated film *Yellow Submarine* followed suit, being lauded more for its songs than its visuals.

Something had clearly begun to go wrong within The Beatles, despite their huge sales and continued acclaim – and by the time of the recording of *The Beatles (The White Album)* in 1968, tensions were at an all-time high, with Lennon focusing on his new wife Yoko Ono and all the musicians wanting to express their widely differing interests elsewhere.

Still, the songs were wondrous, yet again. Late-career Beatles songs written by McCartney included the fresh, upbeat and nicely sarcastic 'Back in the U.S.S.R.'; the curious ska pastiche 'Ob-La-Di, Ob-La-Da'; the beautiful acoustic song 'Blackbird'; the primal heavy metal anthem, 'Helter Skelter'; and the non-album single 'Hey Jude', one of The Beatles' best-known songs to this day. A year later, in 1969, McCartney married photographer Linda Eastman, and their first child

One of the band's final photoshoots. Until Paul announced his departure in April 1970, The Beatles' breakup had been kept quiet for months.

The Beatles' famous rooftop concert – their final live performance together – in January 1969.

Mary – named after his mother – was born later the same year.

Abbey Road, the last Beatles album released while the quartet were still together, was a mixed bag to say the least. Its B-side, a single flow of songs, was McCartney's idea, but the first side has many high points too, including 'Oh! Darling' and the instantly-recognisable bass riff which anchors 'Come Together'. Harrison was on amazing form on this LP, contributing 'Here Comes the Sun' and 'Something', and Lennon delivered the astounding 'I Want You (She's So Heavy)', so most of McCartney's brilliance is confined to the medley – see 'Golden Slumbers' and 'Carry That Weight' for evidence. Just one warning – avoid McCartney's massively annoying 'Maxwell's Silver Hammer' at all costs. The man wasn't perfect, after all. Not that he would have cared what we think.

Although Lennon had effectively 'left' The Beatles several months before, this was not divulged to the public while manager Allen Klein

"Freed of the shackles that bound him to the biggest band of all time, Macca had the world at his feet."

concluded some business deals. By 1970 McCartney had had enough. Disgusted by Klein's machinations and wanting to record solo work, he publicly quit The Beatles on 10 April 1970. The band formally dissolved at the end of the year.

As for *Let It Be*, released a month after the split? The songs were up to their usual high standard, but the production – including unnecessary strings – was the result of a messy, conflicted set of instructions from the group's belligerent new manager Allan Klein and the producer Phil Spector. McCartney's 'Get Back' and 'The Long and Winding Road' still inspire affection among his fans, but his Beatles swansong – and perhaps the song for which he will be most remembered – is the title track, a true anthem for the ages. Not a bad way to leave the stage, eh?

Freed of the shackles that bound him to the biggest band of all time, McCartney – still only 27 years old in 1970 – now had the world at his feet. It was time for him, literally as it turned out, to spread his wings. ✦

Getty

Get Back

The documentary series *The Beatles: Get Back* has given viewers a deeper insight into the band's 1969 *Let It Be* sessions.

McCARTNEY'S MASTERSTROKES

PART I

With an early career full of dizzying highs, we pick some of Macca's greatest artistic moments from his Beatles' era…

It came suddenly...

Let's kick this off in style. 'Yesterday', which appeared on the *Help!* album in 1965 and then as a US single and UK EP track, is said to be the subject of over 2,000 cover versions. We're not really sure why, as it's rather difficult to play, sing and orchestrate. The secret of this huge hit's appeal lies in its earworm melody and the heartstring-twanging emotions that it evokes in the listener, we reckon – and only a genius like McCartney could come up with it.

"Tres bien ensemble!"

'Michelle', part of a long tradition of writing songs so that blokes would buy them for their girlfriends of the same name (see 'Angie' by The Rolling Stones, 'Carol' by Chuck Berry and so on), is unusual for the mid-Sixties in that half of it was sung in French. Macca did a decent job of pronouncing the Gallic vocabulary, as opposed to the German version of 'I Want to Hold Your Hand', retitled 'O Gib Mir Deine Hand', which we suggest that you don't check out.

Jar-jar thinks

The saddest song ever written is McCartney's 'Eleanor Rigby', in which he – accompanied only by a string ensemble – warbles plaintively about the miserable life and unheralded death of the title character. The image that resonates most strongly is encapsulated by the line 'Wearing the face that she keeps in a jar by the door'. What kind of jar? Does it have a lid? Why is it by the door? Which door? These are the questions that only the greatest songwriters make you ask yourself.

Paul takes the stage solo to sing 'Yesterday' on *Blackpool Night Out* in August 1965.

Words: Joel McIver. Images: Getty; Alamy/Mirrorpix (left); www.freepik.com

Octave frenzy

'Paperback Writer', a breezy, uptempo story of how McCartney wants to be a novelist, features a couple of crazy, finger-twisting fills on the bass guitar. These occur at 0'13", 1'02" and later in the song and comprise octave notes – a higher version of the original note, for the non-musicians among us. They're extremely funky, not that you'd know from the accompanying video, in which The Beatles stand around looking completely bored out of their minds.

The Beatles perform 'Paperback Writer' on *Top of the Pops* in June 1966.

"We all live in a yellow submarine..." (Just *try* to get it out of your head!)

Noise annoys

Two McCartney-penned songs are deeply annoying, but you can't help but sing them. One is 'Yellow Submarine', the other is 'Maxwell's Silver Hammer' – and make no mistake, just by reading their titles, you'll be singing them in your head for the rest of today. But it takes a special kind of talent to make lyrics, and melodies, so insanely catchy that you walk around humming them for ages. We genuinely tip our hats to Macca for that.

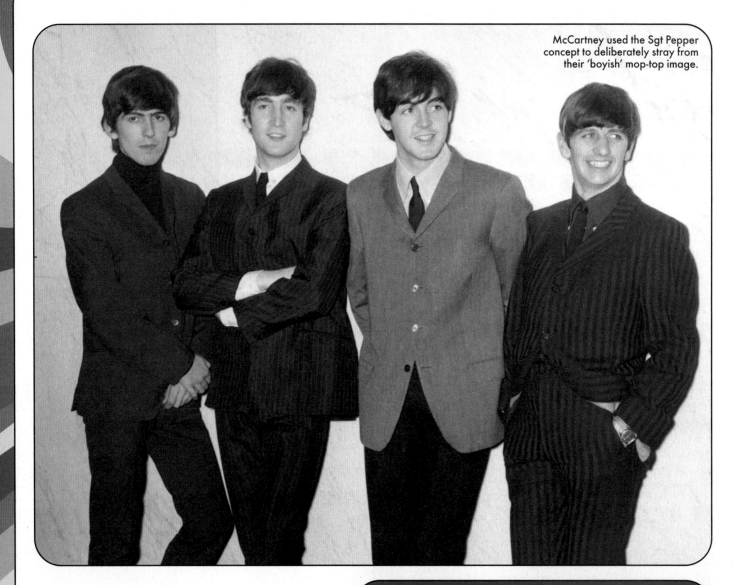

McCartney used the Sgt Pepper concept to deliberately stray from their 'boyish' mop-top image.

"We really hated that fucking four little mop-top boys approach. We were not boys. We were men."

Paul McCartney

From boy to man

In 1966 Paul McCartney was 23 and sick of being treated like a kid. As he later explained, "We were fed up with being The Beatles. We really hated that fucking four little mop-top approach. We were not boys, we were men... And we thought of ourselves as artists rather than just performers." How did he prove this? By conceiving and kickstarting the *Sgt Pepper* album, the defining LP of an era. Yep, he grew up all right.

A bit on the side

Just before the recording of *Sgt Pepper's Lonely Hearts Club Band*, McCartney composed a couple of themes for the soundtrack of the 1966 film, *The Family Way*. The songs, written in collaboration with Beatles producer George Martin, secured him a prestigious Ivor Novello Award for Best Instrumental Theme. Not bad for a bit of work on your day off.

"Bill-eee Sheeeears!"

Sgt. Pepper's Lonely Hearts Club Band, released in 1967, was based on McCartney's concept of a travelling circus, and as such was rock's first concept album. Various animal noises permeated the songs on the LP; a fictional character called Billy Shears was designated to run the show; the band didn't sing about drugs on 'Lucy in the Sky with Diamonds', although everybody thought they did; and Ringo sang a song, bless him.

LEFT: Paul came up with the idea behind the iconic *Sgt Pepper* concept and its aesthetic, which was inspired by Edwardian-era military bands.

"Will Pokemon eat Superman?"

Sgt Pepper's last song, 'A Day in the Life', ends with an infinite loop made up of silly noises. Play that backwards and it sounds exactly like "Will Pokemon eat Superman?" When you've stopped chuckling, replay the song and enjoy McCartney's classic stoner composition, the middle part in which he remarks "Woke up, fell out of bed, dragged a comb across my head". Later he says "I went upstairs and had a smoke," and we believe him.

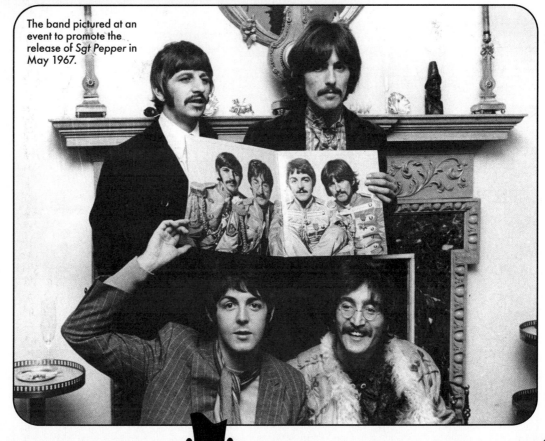

The band pictured at an event to promote the release of *Sgt Pepper* in May 1967.

Paul pictured during the filming of *Magical Mystery Tour* in September 1967.

Learn to fly

Johann Sebastian Bach's 'Bourée In E Minor' was the theme for the beautiful acoustic song 'Blackbird', on which McCartney performs a fingerstyle picking technique taught to him by the Scottish singer Donovan. Apart from some random birdsong, there's nothing on there except Macca's emotional vocal and that wondrous guitar figure. The man had so much talent, it was ridiculous. Bach didn't sue McCartney because he'd been dead for 218 years by the time 'Blackbird' came out.

Mac in the (former) U.S.S.R. – Paul in Moscow before his first ever Russian concert, May 2003.

Those Moscow girls...

'Back in the U.S.S.R.' (1968) is brilliant on every single level. Musically, it's as catchy as hell – who can forget those falsetto 'ooh-way-ooh' backing vocals? Lyrically, it's raunchy as all get-out; Macca is looking for a Russian girlfriend and will not be stopped. Culturally, it's brilliant; the whole thing is a massive mockery of The Beach Boys and their silly, gung-ho 'Back in the U.S.A.'. Politically, it's dynamite; which other rock band was singing the praises of the Soviet Union – albeit ironically – at the height of the Cold War?

Silver screenings

Look, the *Magical Mystery Tour* and *Yellow Submarine* movies may have been mildly irritating in parts and far less than the talents of their creators deserved, but put them in context. How many films did you or I write and (mostly) direct by the time we were 25 years old? None, that's how many – and we weren't also making a series of hit albums at the same time. Macca deserves huge respect for being creative in multiple areas of endeavour.

Classical gas (part 1)

So you've written the most heart-breaking breakup song ever and called it 'For No One'. Who needs regular instruments anyway? Break out the clavichord and French horn for extra baroque'n'roll. Note that his bandmates John Lennon and George Harrison didn't contribute to this song – Macca wasn't sharing this one...

"Mr. Epstein"

Young Paul McCartney always seemed to stay humble, at least in public. After manager Brian Epstein died in 1967, McCartney was keen to keep The Beatles rolling without losing momentum. There is footage of him from the *Let It Be* sessions, telling the others, "We've been very negative since Mr Epstein passed away... we were always fighting [his] discipline a bit, but it's silly to fight that discipline if it's our own", for all the world like a polite schoolboy.

Acid daze

Using drugs for their creative potential rather than because he just wanted to get off his face, McCartney explained that taking acid made him a better and more tolerant person. Later, he packed it in like most sensible people do ("I grew out of it") and in later life was acutely aware that talking about drugs in any positive way was both difficult and ill-advised in the era of smack and skunk.

The band and Yoko Ono pictured during the *Let It Be* sessions. Paul stepped up to try and fill Epstein's shoes after the latter's untimely death.

Getty (left); Alexander Nemenov/AFP via Getty Images (top right); Everett Collection Inc/Alamy (lower right); www.freepik.com

Mastering the 'tache

Picture the scene. It's December 1965 and Macca is riding a moped at some speed. Losing control, he falls off. "I looked at the ground, and it seemed to take a few minutes to think, 'Ah, too bad – I'm going to smack that pavement with my face!'" he later remembered. Left with a scar on his upper lip, our careless driver decided to grow a moustache to hide his embarrassment. Liking the look, the other Beatles soon followed suit, in what was widely thought to be a revolutionary, pre-hippie embracing of facial hair. Of course, we know the truth...

Paul pictured in April 1967, sporting a superb 'tache.

Taking the high road

John Lennon gave a landmark interview to *Rolling Stone* publisher Jann Wenner in 1970, showcasing the ex-Beatle's irritable side. Complaining about more or less everything that The Beatles had ever done, Lennon reserved most of his spite for McCartney. Of *Let It Be*, he whined: "That film was set up by Paul for Paul. That is one of the main reasons The Beatles ended. I can't speak for George, but I pretty damn well know we got fed up of being side-men for Paul." To his credit, McCartney didn't take the bait; in later life he always spoke warmly about his buddy.

Lennon's 1970 *Rolling Stone* interview revealed his brutally honest thoughts on The Beatles' breakup.

Mirrorpix via Getty Images (top left); Getty (lower left); Alamy (right); www.freepik.com

"In the press, they really wanted me to come out and slam John back... But I believe keep cool and that sort of thing passes over."

McCartney discussing his response to Lennon's scathing 1970 *Rolling Stone* interview

Not dying

In October 1969, stupid rumours abounded that McCartney had died in a car crash three years previously – and even better, that he had been replaced by a stand-in. These bizarre conspiracy theories were soundly quashed when *Life* magazine featured him on its cover the following month. The caption was 'Paul is still with us', for anyone in doubt.

Betcha can't play this

'Come Together' is such a popular song that few of us ever stop to think that there's hardly anything to it. For the intro and verses, the song is essentially held together by Macca's elastic bass riff, which we can't easily describe in words other than 'Bah-doom-bah, doobie *doo*-doo'. You know the one...

LEFT: The orchestral sections of *Abbey Road's* epic B-side medley were produced by McCartney and George Martin.

Strings theory

The song medley on the B-side of the *Abbey Road* album is largely McCartney's, and if you wanted to isolate a single amazing moment in that 16-minute chunk of brilliance, we recommend listening to the surge of strings immediately after the line "Once there was a way..." in 'Golden Slumbers'. It brings us to happy tears, every time.

See ya!

We hate to say it, but publicly quitting The Beatles in April 1970 was probably the smartest move McCartney ever made. His relationship with Lennon was at a low ebb, and manager Allen Klein (who essentially the devil in human form) had forced the band to keep their split secret while he tied up loose ends and Beatles business deals. By announcing that he was walking away from the Fab Four, Paul freed himself, his former chum Lennon – and his two other bandmates Harrison and Starr, essentially good blokes caught in the middle – to go off and do their own thing. That must have taken serious courage. What's more, McCartney shouldered much of the blame for the breakup in the years since, despite Lennon being the first one to leave.

LEFT: Although the band had already been drifting apart to pursue solo projects, Paul's announcement marked The Beatles' official break up.

"Say cheese!"

The late Linda Eastman was a photographer who fancied John Lennon, but she soon realised her error. "It was John who interested me at the start. He was my Beatle hero," she once said. "But when I met him the fascination faded fast, and I found it was Paul I liked." She was a good-looking woman by anyone's standards – but she wasn't a model, a fact that the gossiping idiots of the world squawked loud and clear when McCartney married her in 1969. The couple proved them irrelevant by enjoying a happy marriage until Linda's untimely death from cancer in 1998.

Paul met photographer Linda Eastman in May 1967, and the couple married in March 1969.

Twelve gold bars

'Get Back' sang McCartney in 1969, looking in the rear-view mirror at the classic rock'n'roll song structure and incorporating it into the song. For the musicians among us, this classic chord sequence is defined as I-IV-V; for everyone else, this is known as a 12-bar and will be familiar to you from around a gazillion songs that you know and love. Revisiting this structure was an exercise in nostalgic brilliance.

Helter pay

Some learned thinkers say that heavy metal began with Black Sabbath in 1970. Others disagree and attribute the birth of the genre to The Beatles, and specifically to McCartney's indisputably heavy 'Helter Skelter', released in 1968, although still others point to earlier recordings by Jimi Hendrix and The Kinks as the point when the world started headbanging. Whatever the truth, 'Helter Skelter' is a truly memorable bit of heaviosity – and the fact that it was co-opted in 1969 by the murderous Manson Family shouldn't matter a jot.

"I didn't instigate the split. John walked into a room one day and said 'I am leaving The Beatles'... For a few months we had to pretend."

McCartney speaking about The Beatles' split in a 2021 interview for BBC Radio 4

Don't make it bad

What song is so big, so iconic and so damn singable that the writer is asked to perform it as the very last number of the biggest concert ever held? The answer is, of course, is 'Let It Be' – inspired by a dream Paul had about his late mother. Although, as we'll discover later (see page 80), the 1985 event at which McCartney performed it wasn't quite as smooth an operation as he would have liked...

Paul salutes the audience during Live Aid at Wembley Stadium on 13 July 1985.

"

One of my biggest thrills for me still is sitting down with a guitar or a piano and just out of nowhere trying to make a song happen.

"

Paul McCartney

CBS via Getty Images

Chapter 2
PRESS TO PLAY

Getty

STRUM TOGETHER

Sir Paul is a singer, a songwriter, an activist and an icon – but also a master musician. Let's salute his guitar-slinging skills...

Genius doesn't have to be in plain sight. It can be hidden, disguised or simply overshadowed – as in the case of Sir Paul McCartney, who has done so much else in his career that it's easy to forget just how advanced a musician he is. You wouldn't say the same about, say, Elton John, whose expert piano playing is very much to the front of his personality.

Neither could you fail to notice the unearthly guitar playing of Eric Clapton, for example; the very act of being a virtuoso defines ol' Slowhand more than anything else.

In the case of McCartney, however, you might define him as 'co-leader of The Beatles', 'the most famous rock star in the world', 'an incredible singer-songwriter' or 'a spokesperson for a

Paul poses at an organ on the set of the movie *Help!*

generation' – but you probably wouldn't say that his biggest achievement is being a dab hand with a C-sharp minor chord.

This omission is understandable, but it's worth exploring just how and where McCartney excels as a musician, because his musicianship underpins everything he's ever done. If he hadn't picked up a guitar as a kid, he wouldn't have met John Lennon, he wouldn't have become a star, he wouldn't have closed Live Aid and he wouldn't be a spokesperson for vegetarianism and a campaigner for landmine awareness. All this stems from him being a musician.

It all started with Little Richard, reasonably enough. More or less any child born in the years of the Second World War, and who had at least a passing interest in pop music, would have had their mind blown by Richard Penniman – as no-one ever calls him – when he blasted his way onto British TV and radio in the mid-Fifties. His two huge hits, 'Tutti Frutti' (1955) and 'Long Tall

> ## "If Paul hadn't picked up a guitar as a kid, he wouldn't have met John Lennon."

Sally' ('56), were based on Richard's extravagant vocals – not sung but shrieked, to the horror of Frank Sinatra-loving parents everywhere. The young McCartney loved this display of showmanship and wrote 'I'm Down' in 1965 as a successful Little Richard homage.

Add the emerging presence of Elvis Presley, Buddy Holly, Carl Perkins and Chuck Berry to the average radio playlist in the McCartney household, and it's little wonder that in 1957 the 14-year-old Paul picked up his first guitar, a Framus Zenith acoustic, for £15. His guitar skills evolved fairly quickly: if we jump forward only three years to The Quarrymen's first gigs at the Cavern Club in Liverpool and the Star-Club in Hamburg, Macca was already holding down competent rhythm guitar parts for hours on end.

Of course, as a musician, McCartney will always be remembered most as a bass player – which is remarkable for several compelling reasons. One, the bass guitar was regarded as the

Getty

Recording the bass in the studio, circa 1967.

Paul rehearsing a song at the piano with Welsh singer-songwriter Mary Hopkin (right), for an appearance on the TV show *Magpie* presented by Pete Brady (left).

Make no mistake, Paul McCartney was a pioneer on bass: there is no other accurate way to describe him. His predecessor in The Quarrymen, Stuart Sutcliffe, quit the band in 1961, obliging McCartney to take up the instrument. George Harrison was too good a guitarist to make the switch, and the group's then-leader John Lennon was presumably deemed too important to be a mere bass player. Once The Beatles were established, McCartney found himself lumbered with a Höfner 500/1, or 'violin bass'; this cheap instrument didn't make particularly impressive noises, but it was pretty much all there was if you couldn't afford the aforementioned Precision, an expensive American import.

All credit to him: rather than complain, or settle for boring bass parts, Macca knuckled down to the task of making the bass sound interesting. This wasn't easy given the dull tones of the Höfner, and what's more, the job was made far tougher by the fact that he had to play and sing lead and harmony vocals at the same time – often in high-speed rock songs, and often for six hours at a stretch over a night at the Star-Club. Aged just 18 in 1961, McCartney pulled it off spectacularly.

If you want evidence, head straight for 'I Saw Her Standing There' (1963), on which he delivered a speedy rock'n'roll line 'borrowed' from Chuck Berry, as he later acknowledged. The violin bass was incapable of delivering thunderous bass tones, so instead he played a zippy mid-register line that stood out nicely. Then there's 'Please Please Me', where he did what all the most sensible bass players do and left gaps between the bass notes, allowing them to stand out more clearly – quite a self-aware move for a musician just out of his teens. By 1963 he was playing fast notes in sync with the guitar lines ('All My Loving') and piano ('Money [That's What I Want]') and honing a very precise style.

least cool instrument in the Fifties, at least in rock and roll bands. The bass was usually handed to the band member who could most easily be persuaded or bullied into playing it. Two, bass amps lacked power, and most bass guitars – the hallowed Fender Precision aside, which few musicians could afford – were basically junk. Three, you couldn't get any clarity out of the strings – and even if you could, your amp couldn't make you loud enough to cut through the guitars. If you were the bass player, you were the butt of many a joke. It was no fun.

Four bass players changed all that. The first was James Jamerson, Motown's in-house studio bassist, who recorded bass on pretty much every

American soul song that mattered from 1959 onwards. McCartney paid tribute to Jamerson, both verbally and in the funky, soulful bass parts that he recorded for so many Beatles songs. The second was McCartney himself, as we'll see in a moment; the third was The Who's John Entwistle; and the fourth was Jack Bruce of Cream. Both of these latter bassists came to prominence around 1965, three years after Macca and seven years after Jamerson. Both enjoyed a newfound freedom as bassists. Their instrument had finally reached a place where it could be as expressive – and as important in a band – as the guitars. Who was responsible for this new spirit of bass-friendliness in rock music? Take a wild guess.

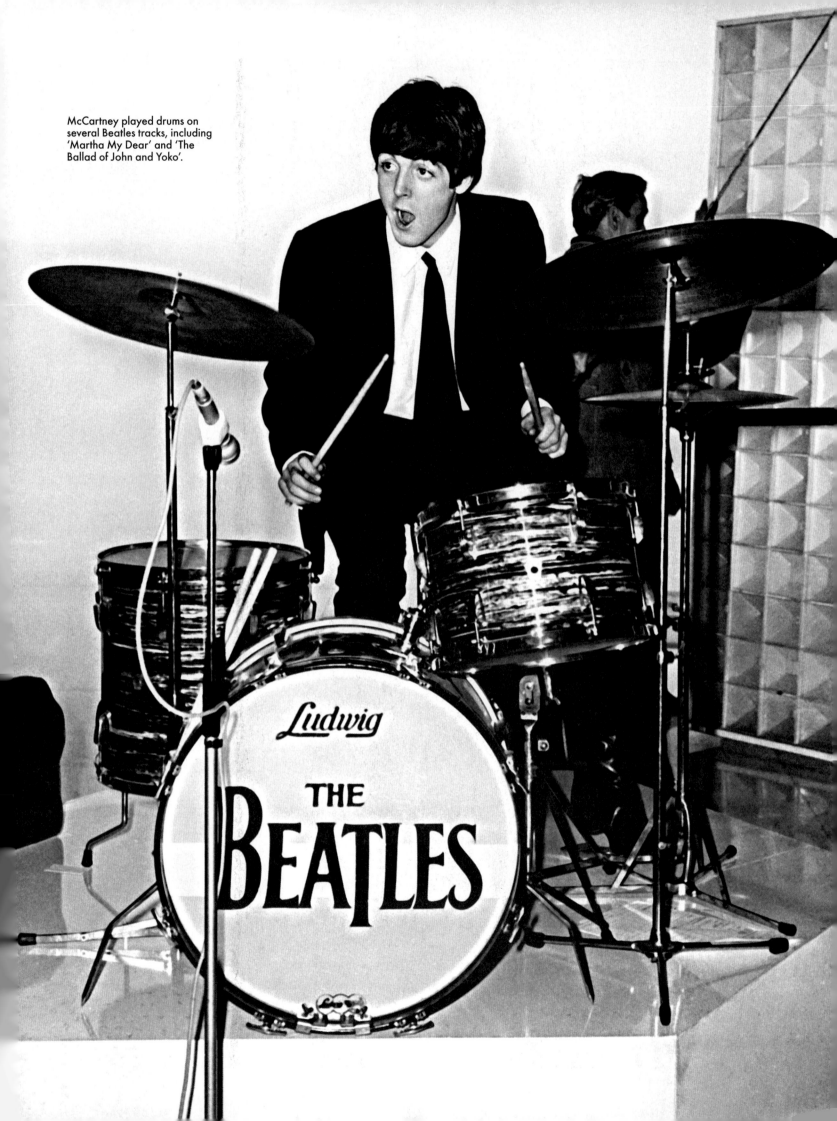

McCartney played drums on several Beatles tracks, including 'Martha My Dear' and 'The Ballad of John and Yoko'.

Through The Beatles rock'n'roll years, let's say up to the release of *Help!* in '65, McCartney's bass parts were known for being fast but supportive; by the middle of the decade – and indeed the band's career – he had switched to a more robust bass, a Rickenbacker 4001S, and begun to elevate his lines' melodic content. Simple bass parts still abounded in his repertoire, in order to properly serve songs such as 'Ticket to Ride' and the descending part which anchored 'Nowhere Man', but as time passed the bass began to be more and more important. By *Revolver* (1966), he was all over songs like 'She Said She Said', 'And Your Bird Can Sing' and 'Taxman', in which he echoes the lightning-speed central guitar riff with little apparent effort.

By 1967's *Sgt Pepper's Lonely Hearts Club Band*, the die was cast. McCartney's bass was now firmly a part of the new psychedelic rock sound, dominating the mix – unsurprisingly, as the album concept was largely his – and a major part of 'Lucy in the Sky with Diamonds', 'Fixing a Hole', 'When I'm Sixty-Four' and the non-album single 'Penny Lane'. Subsequent albums continued to turn up bass gems, including 'Ob-La-Di, Ob-La-Da' on *The Beatles*, 'Something' and 'Come Together' on *Abbey Road* and 'Get Back' on *Let It Be*.

Macca's best-known bass riff is almost certainly the figure that dominates 'Come Together', and it's arguable that he overplayed on 'Something'. We know this because of an anecdote he told about a filthy look directed his way during the song's recording by its composer, Harrison. Sometimes, too much bass is really too much, after all, and in the Wings and solo years, he focused less on melodic bass parts, preferring to concentrate on supporting the songs and delivering vocals. As the sole frontman where his previous band had featured two, this was understandable.

Note that McCartney sometimes played guitar in The Beatles. His choice was often acoustic, which made sense given his interest in writing ballads and the presence of the two electric axe-playing hotheads in the band – see 'Blackbird' for his most notable performance. 'Yesterday', 'Michelle', 'Mother Nature's Son' and others including 'Rocky Raccoon' feature less extravagant acoustic parts, but they're not meant to be upfront. Instead, they're simple, emotional and perfectly gauged as vehicles for the message of the lyrics.

This doesn't mean that Macca couldn't rock out on guitar when he wanted to. He played a chaotic solo in 'Drive My Car', another on 'Taxman' – appropriately, as the song was meant to express resentment – and most memorably, the guitar squeals on 'Sgt Pepper's Lonely Hearts Club Band'. There really was no limit to what he could do, and in the post-Epstein era when he essentially directed the band, McCartney was allowed to get away with more or less whatever he chose.

A quick word in closing about Macca's other musical skills. He's an excellent piano player,

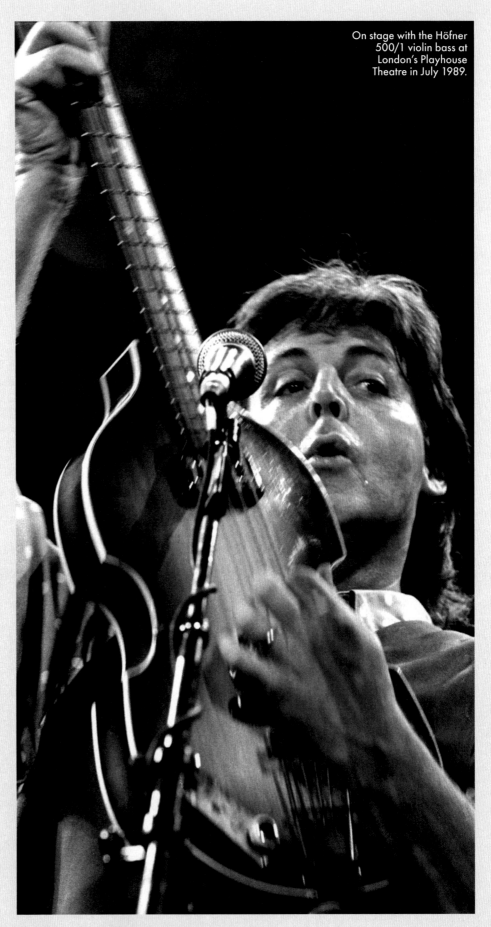

On stage with the Höfner 500/1 violin bass at London's Playhouse Theatre in July 1989.

McCartney pictured on acoustic guitar during the studio sessions for *Let It Be*.

"McCartney's best-known bass riff is the figure that dominates 'Come Together'."

having composed on the instrument on a more-or-less constant basis throughout The Beatles' career. The wonderful descending chord sequence of 'For No One' is his, as is the upbeat swirl of notes on 'Hello, Goodbye'; the instantly recognisable piano parts of 'Hey Jude' and 'Let It Be' are McCartney creations; and his ivories-tinkling on 'The Long and Winding Road' is heartbreaking. As for his piano-playing on 'Lady Madonna', it's pretty much the essence of rock and roll.

Macca also plays drums: is there no end to the man's talents? As well as taking Ringo Starr's place on a number of Fab Four tunes – 'Dear Prudence', 'Back in the U.S.S.R.' and 'The Ballad of John and Yoko' – he nailed all the drum parts on his solo albums *McCartney* (1970), *McCartney II* (1980) and the more recent *McCartney III* (2020). And if you need further evidence of his tub-thumping ability, consider the fact that he played drums on 'Sunday Rain', a song from the Foo Fighters' album *Concrete and Gold* (2017). Yes, Foo Fighters – as in the band led by the most famous drummer in the world, Dave Grohl. You couldn't make it up, could you? ✦

McCartney conducts a 41-piece orchestra during recording sessions for *Sgt Pepper's* 'A Day in the Life'.

Getty; Alamy (top right)

"

My approach to music is rather like the primitive cave artists, who drew without training.

"

Paul McCartney

Maestro Macca

Paul pictured conducting the orchestra during the recording of 'A Day in the Life' in February 1967.

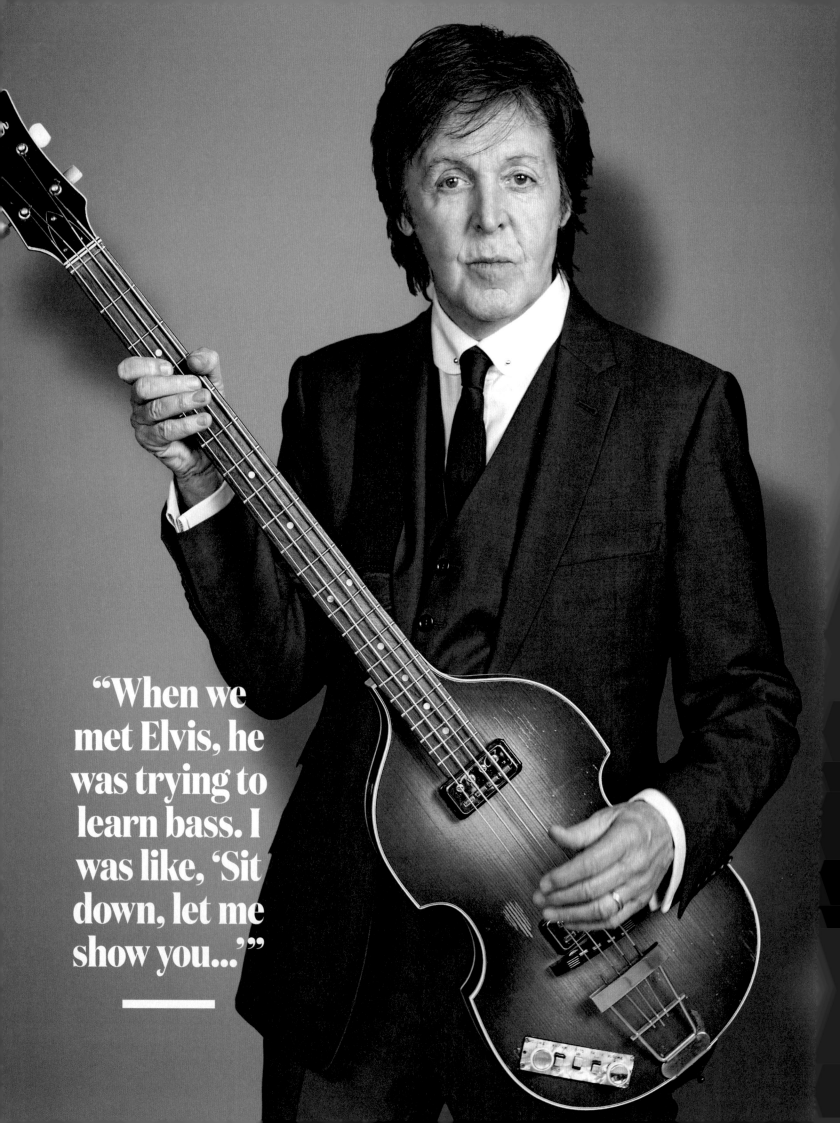

"When we met Elvis, he was trying to learn bass. I was like, 'Sit down, let me show you...'"

FROM THE **Bass** Guitar Magazine ARCHIVES

IN HIS OWN WORDS...

We celebrate of the work of Sir Paul McCartney, the most famous electric bass player of them all, with a classic Macca interview by the great Tony Bacon

I met Paul McCartney for this interview in November 1994 at his studio in East Sussex. It was part of my research for the first edition of *The Bass Book*, and McCartney could not have been more generous, entertaining, and candid in the few hours we spent together. I started by asking him about my favourite period of his bass work with The Beatles, during the making of *Sgt Pepper*…

When you were recording *Sgt Pepper*, you created some great independent lines for the bass.

Yeah, that was really when I got into that. That was probably what ended up being my strongest thing on bass, the independent melodies. On 'Lucy in the Sky with Diamonds', you could easily have had [he sings a root-note version through the first few chords]. It would have been like 'Louie Louie' or something. Whereas I was going [sings the 'Lucy' bass-line], just running through that. It's only really a way of getting from C to F, or whatever, but you get there in an interesting way. That became my thing, doing that.

In the early days, the bass was just something you had to put in the song, but now you seemed to be thinking about being a bass player in your own right.

From the word go, once I got over the fact that I was lumbered with the bass [laughs], I did get quite proud to be a bass player, quite proud of the idea. Once you realised the control you had over the band, you were in control. They can't go anywhere, man. Ha! Power! I then started to identify with other bass players, to talk bass with the guys in the band. In fact, when we met Elvis, he was trying to learn bass, so I was like, 'You're trying to learn bass, are you … son? Sit down, let me show you a few things'. So I was very proud of being the bass player. But as it went on and I got into that melodic thing, that was probably the peak of my interest.

You were responsible for many people thinking of the bass as a much more acceptable instrument, compared to when you were "lumbered" with it back in the early days of the band, when you took over from Stu Sutcliffe.

The British are coming: The Beatles led the British Invasion of the US charts in the Sixties.

Yeah, it became a bit more skillful. I wouldn't personally credit myself, but thanks for that. But I think James Jamerson, him and me, I'd share the credit there. I was nicking a lot off him. That was the thing, though, it did become a lot more of a funky instrument: it was becoming almost like a drum, the rhythmic possibilities. It was very

*Words: Tony Bacon. **Images:** Press image via DawBell (left), Getty (right)*

exciting, that, and it also gave me something to keep me interested. The danger with bass is that everybody else has got the interesting jobs and you're just the last guy to get a part, and literally you get the root notes, two in a bar. But actually… now, I quite like that, I like the simplicity. Sort of country and western bass playing.

It's like you have to learn the complicated stuff in order to…

To come back, that's right, to come back to the nice simple stuff. But as I say, I became very proud to be the bass player in The Beatles. The other thing for me that was hard was because some of these parts were independent melodic parts, it became much more difficult to sing, it was like doing this [pats his head and rubs his stomach]. So I had to put a little special effort into that, which made it very interesting. If you were singing "She was just 17…" and going [sings energetic bass-line], well… that became the skill, I could

just learn [sings 'I Saw Her Standing There' bass-line], nicked from Chuck Berry as I'm sure you know, 'I'm Talking About You'. I've given him credit, though.

In Wings, it rarely seemed to be at the same creative level.

I never quite had the interest that I had during that sort of dream period around *Sgt Pepper*, and *Rubber Soul*, when I was doing something. See, with Wings, I was now the band leader, the business manager, the this, the that… we didn't have Apple, we didn't have [manager Brian] Epstein, we didn't have anything. It was me doing it all. That was the biggest headache. That's difficult. In The Beatles, I'd been free of all of that – we had a manager, we had three other great guys. I could concentrate everything on writing the song, singing harmony with John [Lennon], or playing the bass, pretty much my role, or maybe playing a bit of piano or guitar or something. Other than

that, I really didn't have much to do, so you could put all your energy into that. And I think after that, I sidelined the role of bass, a bit, in favour of the role of frontman. It was not really my favourite thing to do, but there was really nothing else to do. The only alternative was to give up music, that I saw.

Your first basses in The Beatles were the famous Höfners. How did you come to play those?

I found a nice little shop in the centre of Hamburg, near a big department store called Karstadt. And I saw this bass in the window, this violin-shaped Höfner. It was a good price, because my dad had always said I shouldn't do the never-never [buy on credit], but we were earning reasonable money. I liked the Höfner's lightness, too. So I bought it, and I think it was only about 30 quid. I've still got one which is from The Beatles days, one I actually use now on tour, and I've had some technical

Press photos via DawBell

Paul's 1963 Höfner 500/1 (top), still with a '66 setlist taped to the side, and his 1964 Rickenbacker 4001S (bottom), today stripped of its original red finish and later psychedelic daubs

work done on that. Last year, Mandolin Brothers in New York did some serious good work, actually put it in tune for the first time in its life. Usually the E could be in tune but the third fret G was always a little bit sharp – as soon as you'd gone to the third fret it was a little bit sharp. I was using it on a big tour, so it was a bit embarrassing. I hadn't used it for a long time for that reason, but I got it all sorted.

Were you listening to other bass players much? You already mentioned James Jamerson.
Funnily enough, I'd always liked bass. My dad was a musician, and I remember he would give me little sort of lessons, not actual sit-down lessons, but he'd just say something... when there was something on the radio he'd say, 'Hear that down low? That's the bass'. I remember him actually pointing out what a bass was, and he'd do little lessons in harmony. So when I came to The

Beatles, I had a little bit of musical knowledge through him – very amateur. And yes, then I started listening to other bass players, mainly as time went on. Motown, James Jamerson became just my hero, really. I didn't actually know his name until quite recently. Him and Brian Wilson were my two biggest influences. James Jamerson just because he was so good and melodic, and Brian because he went to very unusual places. If you were playing in C, he might stay on the G a lot, just to hold it all back, and again, I started to realise the power you had within the band, not actually vengeful power, just that even though the whole band is going in A you could go in E, and they'd go 'Let us off the hook!' You're actually in control then, an amazing thing. So I sussed that and got particularly interested in playing the bass. Then I took it beyond that. I thought 'If you can do that, what else can you do?' You might even be able to play notes that aren't in the chord. I just started to experiment: what could you do? Well,

maybe you can use different notes. Sevenths instead of the regular notes, or maybe even a little tune through the chords that doesn't exist anywhere else. That idea of an independent melody.

On some Beatles footage you look like you're playing with a plectrum; elsewhere, as though you're playing with your thumb.
I did a bit of both. Mainly, if it was a sort of important gig, I'd nearly always resort to a pick because I feel safer that way. And with recording it helps. The engineers used to like to hear the pick, because then they get the treble end out as well as the bass, and they could do the mix, get it to kick right out. I used to do a bit of both. I was never trained in any styles, so I just picked it up.

How did you get your Rickenbacker bass?
I got it in America. Now we were getting quite famous – obviously once we got to America we

"My dad was a musician, and I remember he would give me little sort of lessons. not actual, sit-down lessons, but when there was something on the radio he'd say, 'Hear that down low? That's the bass.'"

were quite famous – and Mr Rickenbacker said 'Paul, we have a bass'. Oh, great! Freebie! Thank you very much. I became fond of that instrument and then I used to use either that or the Höfner, just to vary it a little bit, and round about the time of *Sgt Pepper* I was definitely using the Rickenbacker quite a lot. It was a slightly different style, and it stayed in tune better, that was the great thing.

I think you started using the Rickenbacker around the time of *Rubber Soul* in 1965, and 'Michelle' always struck me as a good melodic line, quite thought out.
It actually was thought up on the spot. Yeah! Because you didn't have much time. You had to think on your feet, that was the thing. I would never have played 'Michelle' on bass until I had to record the bass-line. Bass isn't an instrument you sit around and sing to – I don't, anyway. But 'Michelle', I remember that line against the descending chords, that was like, oh, a great moment in my life. It's quite a well-known trick to do that, I'm sure jazz players have done that against that descending thing. But wherever I got it from, the back of my brain somewhere said: do that, that'll be nice, it just lays it out a bit more. Just a bit cleverer for the arrangement, it'll sound good on those descending chords.

How long did the Rickenbacker have the psychedelic paint job?
That was around the time of *Magical Mystery Tour*, I got out the old aerosols. Because we were all doing that: George did his guitar, we did the cars. So if you did the cars, you might as well do your guitars. It looked great, and it was just because we were tripping, that's what it was, man. Look at your guitar and you'd trip even more. I sort of grew out of that, like most people did.

I believe you've been looking back at your time in The Beatles for a TV project called *Anthology* [first broadcast in 1995, the year after this interview]. What's that been like?
It's very good. Funniest thing is that we don't always agree on the memories, because it's 30 years ago. So it's hilarious… on camera. There's one bit, Ringo's telling a story, and he says, 'At that point George had a sore throat…' Camera pans to George, George says, 'I thought it was Paul', and the camera pans to me, and I say, 'Well I know it was John.' And I've worked it out since, I say this to people: if Ringo thought it was George, it wasn't Ringo; if George thought it was me, it wasn't George; I thought it was John, so it wasn't me. It must have been John, he was the only one left! But this is funny, for the definitive bloody thing on The Beatles. It's great, you've just got to laugh. It's so human, so real. We forget… who cares? We did some great stuff. Exact analysis was never our bag. And it obviously still isn't! ⬇

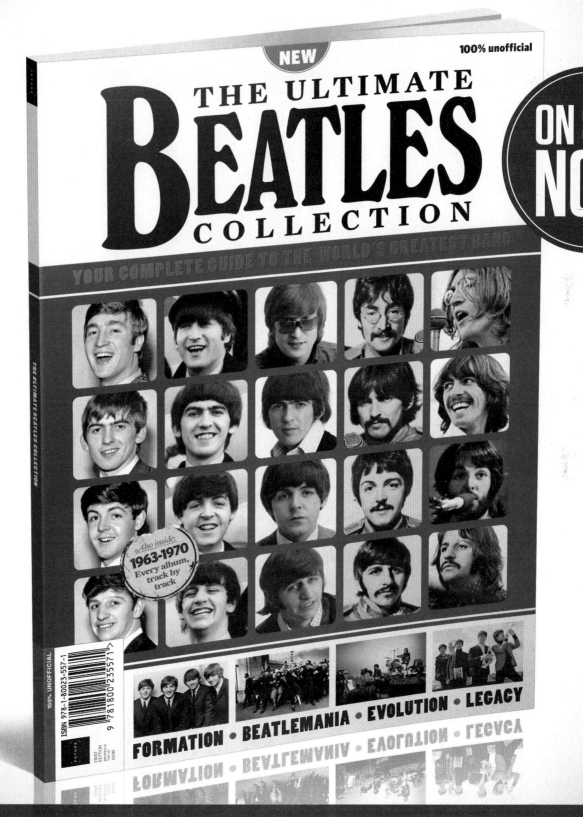

Chapter 3
TWICE IN A LIFETIME

TAKING FLIGHT

What Paul did next: we salute Macca's 20th-century work as a solo artist and with Wings

What do you do when you walk away from the biggest rock band ever formed? You have a choice: quit music entirely, or take a deep breath, start from ground zero and give it another go.

You could argue that the phrase 'giving it another go' is an exact summary of Paul McCartney's 50 years of music-making since the split of The Beatles in 1970. In this feature we're focusing on the first 30 years of that period, a three-decade chunk of creativity in which he was impressively prolific, releasing no fewer than 11 solo albums, seven more with the band Wings,

three as a classical composer, and two with his Fireman collaboration, as well as various miscellaneous projects. And that's just his recording side – he regularly played live, too, touring at stadium level as well as headlining huge one-off events. The man's been busy.

Inevitably, it took McCartney a little while to start firing on all cylinders again after the four-way divorce of the Fab Four. Plagued by depression and embroiled in an existential crisis – as we would all be, in that situation – he was pulled back out of the rabbit-hole by his wife Linda, for whom he wrote 'Maybe I'm Amazed' amid the split. The song appeared on his first solo

Words: Joel McIver. Image: Getty

album, *McCartney*, recorded entirely by him apart from vocals from his ever-supportive missus. The LP was released in April 1970 – in other words, after The Beatles had privately split up, but before the group had legally been dissolved and the news made public.

Now, here's a thing. McCartney's first solo record, along with every single album he's released since then, has always been compared against his work in The Beatles, and come out on the wrong side of that comparison. In a sense, this has been unavoidable. The Beatles' catalogue contains so much gold – and so few misfires, relatively speaking – that no band, including acts as huge as The Rolling Stones, Led Zeppelin, the Sex Pistols, The Smiths, Ed Sheeran or Adele, could hope to match it. That includes McCartney himself, whose solo songwriting is generally regarded as charming at best.

That huge millstone around his neck aside, it should also be noted that McCartney changed his approach a little when he embarked on his solo career. Adjectives such as 'homegrown', 'organic', 'indie' and 'lo-fi' suited his new music down to the ground; picture the man on a Scottish farm, surrounded by wife, kids and livestock and strumming a ditty about how good life is out in the country, and you'll get the picture. This approach wasn't for everyone, least of all fans of The Beatles' high-concept, avant-garde work. Compare the winsome 'Lovely Linda' against the apocalyptic 'A Day in the Life', for example.

Then there was 1971's *Ram*, on whose cover McCartney was pictured with the eponymous mammal: the LP consolidated his image as a millionaire living comfortably off his Beatles royalties with nothing much of note to say. This isn't to say that the songs were bad, or that the musicianship lacked craftsmanship and dedication – the song 'Uncle Albert/Admiral Halsey' was a deserved US Number One – but

after the white heat of his old band, McCartney's output now seemed a little, well, lukewarm.

It took the formation of a full-blown band, Wings, for the critics – never the most supportive audience when it comes to band members who go solo – to take Macca seriously again. Ex-Moody Blues guitarist Denny Laine, drummer Denny Seiwell (what were the chances of two Dennys in the same band?) and McCartney himself made for a seriously talented group of musicians. That said, the addition of Linda as keyboard player provoked some criticism: she was not a trained keys player, and accusations of nepotism were rife.

Still, a low-key debut tour helped win McCartney's critics over. Wisely, he arranged for Wings to play 11 shows at university level, entertaining merely hundreds of music fans. The band – now joined by guitarist Henry McCullough – were on a budget, staying in affordable accommodation, a fact noted by skeptics with approval.

McCartney later explained, "The main thing I didn't want was to come on stage, faced with the whole torment of five rows of press people with little pads, all looking at me and saying, 'Oh well, he's not as good as he was'. So we decided to go out on that university tour which made me less nervous... by the end of that tour I felt ready for something else, so we went into Europe." Twenty-five continental shows later, Wings were now an understood quantity, if not entirely a welcomed one: that would require new music, and convincing music at that.

1971's *Wild Life* LP was a decent debut, but an American chart-topper in 'My Love' really stamped Wings' presence on the world and made their second album *Red Rose Speedway* ('73) a bona fide hit. The band's profile was given a further boost the same year by the enormous success of 'Live and Let Die', the theme song for the James

Wings in 1974, from left to right: Paul, Linda, Jimmy McCulloch, Denny Laine, Geoff Britton.

Paul and Linda recorded *Ram* together in 1970-71.

Paul and Linda at the premiere for *Live and Let Die* in July 1973.

Bond film of the same name. An operatic, highly dynamic composition that managed to combine the usual Bond trademarks with a spellbinding hookline, the song remains one of Macca's finest ever, a fact noted by the heavy metal band Guns N' Roses when they covered it in 1991. The song was nominated for an Academy Award and bagged producer George Martin a Grammy for his orchestral arrangement.

The remainder of the Seventies was a hugely successful period for Wings, who released a series of platinum-selling albums. The first was the Grammy-winning *Band on the Run*, which was inescapable through 1974, remaining on the UK chart for 124 weeks. *Venus and Mars* (1975) and *Wings at the Speed of Sound* (1976) were just as successful despite the group's fluctuating line-up, making Wings a viable concept even to the most hardened cynic. The inclusion of a few Beatles songs in Wings' setlist was a turning-point, making it apparent that McCartney was at peace

> ## *"Band on the Run was inescapable through 1974, remaining on the UK chart for 124 weeks."*

with his past as well as appreciative that fans wanted to hear the songs again.

After an American chart-topping triple live album, *Wings Over America* (1976), it's arguable that Wings peaked. Punk rock was on its way, after all – but that didn't stop McCartney putting out the biggest-selling single of his career, as a Beatle or not. 'Mull of Kintyre', co-written with Denny Laine, was a commercial behemoth, outselling every other song in history until Band Aid's 'Do They Know It's Christmas?' seven years later. 'Mull of Kintyre' is still the most successful non-charity single ever released in the UK, thanks to its heartstring-twanging lyrics about the pleasures of the countryside and its stirring bagpipe parts.

Although *London Town* (1978) supplied another US Number One in 'With a Little Luck', and *Back to the Egg* ('79) featured a supergroup including Pete Townshend (The Who), David Gilmour (Pink Floyd), Gary Brooker (Procol Harum) and John

Paul and Linda at
High Park Farm in
Kintyre, Scotland.

Paul Jones and John Bonham of Led Zeppelin, the writing was on the wall for Wings. After a second solo LP, *McCartney II*, was a major hit in 1980, Macca disbanded Wings the following year.

Was this a wise move? That's debatable. The Eighties were a mixed decade for McCartney, as it was for so many musicians of a certain vintage. Now sporting a mullet and beginning to look disturbingly like your dad, he embarked on a series of projects that were rather cringeworthy.

The best of these was 'Ebony and Ivory', a 1982 collaboration with Stevie Wonder, but even so, its lyrical metaphor was a touch hamfisted.

Two more collaborations in the early Eighties, this time with Michael Jackson, were also commercially successful. 'The Girl Is Mine' and 'Say Say Say' had their charms, for sure, but they were supremely bland: was this really the same Paul McCartney who had recorded 'Helter Skelter' and 'Back in the U.S.S.R.'?

It got worse, with the ultra-sugary 'Pipes of Peace' a massive hit in 1983 among grandparents worldwide. The following year, McCartney wrote, produced and starred in a musical film called *Give My Regards to Broad Street*, described by *Variety* as "characterless, bloodless, and pointless". The song 'No More Lonely Nights' was a pleasantly inoffensive ballad, for sure, but then McCartney made the curious decision to release a juvenile Rupert Bear-themed song called 'We All Stand

McCartney sported one of the most famous mullets of the Seventies and Eighties.

Mirrorpix via Getty Images (left); Getty (right)

Together' in 1984 – also known as the 'Frog Song' – perhaps his worst ever creative move.

Fortunately, things began to look up for our man after this point, with the moderately entertaining film and song *Spies Like Us*, both released in 1985. In July, the biggest live gig there has ever been or will ever be, Live Aid, took place – and while much has been written about its role in turning rock music into corporate fodder for inefficient charities, it cannot be denied that asking McCartney to close the show with 'Let It Be' was a masterstroke of the highest order. The fact that his microphone wasn't working for the first few seconds of the song somehow added to the surreal charm of this massive event.

That was it – the turning-point that was needed. McCartney, and his fans, were reminded of what an icon he had been, and he set about making good on that legacy with a series of decent records. *Press to Play* (1986) made it clear to listeners that he still was a rocker at heart, and the 1988 LP *CHOBA B CCCP* – literally *"Back in the*

Paul performs to a record-breaking crowd in Rio de Janeiro, April 1990.

On stage at the Here, There and Everywhere tribute concert, which was held in honour of Linda on 10 April 1999 after her untimely death.

In the studio in June 1979, following the release of *Back to the Egg*.

"I used to think that all my Wings stuff was second-rate, but I began to meet younger kids, not kids from my Beatle generation, who would say, 'We really love this song'."

Paul McCartney

U.S.S.R." – confounded expectations by being released only in the Soviet Union: a provocative move in the pre-glasnost era. He appeared on a charity version of 'Ferry Cross the Mersey' in 1989, raising funds for the Hillsborough Disaster Appeal, and entered the Nineties with the well-received *Flowers in the Dirt*, a collaborative project with Elvis Costello.

A second career peak came about at this time, with the McCartney band breaking a record by playing for the largest paying stadium audience in history on 21 April 1990. An astounding 184,000 people watched him play at Maracanã Stadium in Rio de Janeiro in Brazil, and the subsequent live album *Tripping the Live Fantastic* consolidated his newfound stature. He punctuated the rest of the decade with solo and classical albums, the first of these commissioned in 1991 by the Royal Liverpool Philharmonic Society. The piece *Liverpool Oratorio* was his first venture into classical, and earned him a 1995 Honorary Fellowship of the Royal College of Music.

Other high points of the Nineties included an appearance on *MTV Unplugged*, two albums with Youth of Killing Joke as a musical duo called The Fireman, and more solo albums every year or two. Live albums kept fans happy and the McCartney brand on people's minds, but the decade – and century – came to a sad end with the death of Linda, who succumbed to breast cancer in 1998 at the age of only 56.

McCartney appeared at a tribute event, the Concert for Linda, at the Royal Albert Hall in London on 10 April 1999, and sought solace in counselling. His fans shared his grief – and we asked ourselves what the future held for him. ✈

Antonio Scorza/AFP via Getty Images (top left): Getty

Band on the Run

Wings pictured at Abbey Road Studios to record *Venus and Mars* in November 1974. From left to right: Geoff Britton, Paul and Linda McCartney, Denny Laine and Jimmy McCulloch.

McCARTNEY'S MASTERSTROKES

PART 2

Yesterday no more – let's take a look at some of the many highlights of Macca's post-Beatles career and personal life…

'Live and Let Die'

Bond theme tunes aren't usually that good, if you ask us, although there are at least three notable exceptions – Shirley Bassey's 'Diamonds Are Forever' (1971), Paul McCartney's 'Live and Let Die' (1973) and Chris Cornell's astounding 'You Know My Name' from *Casino Royale* (2006). Of these, the first is the most operatic, the third the most technically impressive, and the second the most viscerally exciting. Here, McCartney executes a masterclass in the dynamics of tension and release in songwriting: when the tempo suddenly accelerates, it's impossible not to play air guitar, bass, piano or drums.

"It's a masterclass in the dynamics of tension and release in songwriting..."

The video for 'Uncle Albert/Admiral Halsey'

A high point of *Ram* (1971), this song was a major hit – and for obvious reasons, as it's a bit of yacht-rock wonderfulness – but if you really want to know where Macca's head was at during this period of his career, head to YouTube for the accompanying video clip. It's essentially the bucolic, 'getting your head together in the country' escape fantasy that we all have. Paul, Linda and two of their kids are pictured on the farm, on the beach and generally having fun in a manner far removed from the celeb hurly-burly of Beatles-world.

'Live and Let Die' became the first Bond theme to be nominated for Best Original Song at the Academy Awards.

Words: Joel McIver. Images: Getty; www.freepik.com

Continuing to take the high road

John Lennon, creative genius and man of peace though he undoubtedly was, could also be something of a git at times, judging by the many unpleasant things he said about McCartney between The Beatles' split in 1970 and his untimely death a decade later. To his massive, ongoing credit, Macca rarely – if ever – retaliated, quietly setting the record straight in his biography but otherwise refusing to hit back at Lennon's accusations. Fortunately, the last communication between the two men – a phone call not long before Lennon was murdered – was a friendly one, according to McCartney, which is presumably some consolation.

Yoko Ono pictured at the reopening of the renovated Indica Gallery in 2006, where she first met John Lennon.

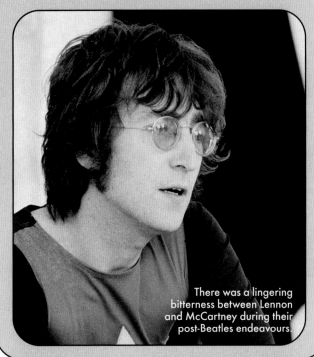

There was a lingering bitterness between Lennon and McCartney during their post-Beatles endeavours.

Art attack

A lover and practitioner of fine art as well as music, Paul McCartney helped out with the renovation of the Indica Gallery in Mason's Yard, London, in 1965. A writer, Barry Miles, had co-founded the venue – as well as the *International Times*, an underground newspaper with which McCartney also assisted – and it was at the Gallery that John Lennon first met Yoko Ono. Miles went on to write Macca's authorised biography, *Many Years from Now*, in 1997.

Getting Linda on keyboards

Linda McCartney, as the wife of pretty much the most famous bloke on the planet for the second half of her life, was often the recipient of mean-mannered jibes and criticisms from 'haters', as nobody called them back then. Undeterred and unbowed, she joined Wings as the keyboard player, even though she couldn't play the instrument particularly well. She and the hubby were criticised by various idiots for this, but you know what? Screw 'em. Linda joining Wings was actually a hell of a punk thing to do.

The McCartneys on stage with Wings in Liverpool, November 1979.

Paul and Linda pictured together in December 1972.

> "It was for Linda and was about her. It was to try and get a little deeper into a love song... The sort of stuff that you don't say to a girl except in a song. I think a lot of people relate to it."

McCartney discussing 'Maybe I'm Amazed' in a 2001 *Billboard* interview

'Maybe I'm Amazed'

Even before The Beatles went their separate ways, McCartney was being creative in his own right. One of his first songs, 1970's 'Maybe I'm Amazed', was inspired by his wife Linda, who had helped to lift him out of the depression that he was feeling. You and I would be depressed as well if we'd walked away from the biggest band in the world – but we'd feel better if the world's greatest songwriter wrote a little ditty for us, too.

Going platinum

Name a singer who quit a major band, went solo and became hugely successful. Ozzy Osbourne, George Michael and Harry Styles maybe? It's a very short list – but Paul McCartney is definitely at the top of it, and what's more, he was the first musician to do it. Wings had seven platinum-selling albums in less than a decade. Who else could possibly pull that off?

Getty; www.freepik.com

'The Girl Is Mine'

On paper, a duet between McCartney and the late Michael Jackson, then about to hit big with his planet-sized *Thriller* album, didn't sound particularly promising. However, 'The Girl Is Mine' – a bit of mild banter between the two megastars about which of them should pursue an unidentified female – was a massive hit in 1982, reaching the Top 10 in both the US and UK. A second duet, 'Say Say Say', was released the following year and wasn't quite as good, but y'know, you can't have everything.

LEFT: McCartney and Michael Jackson posing together at a recording studio in 1983.

BELOW: Paul, Denny Laine and Linda pictured with the Campbeltown Pipe Band while filming a promotional video for 'Mull of Kintyre'.

Buying the farm

Acquiring a chunk of Scotland was a clever move, and not just because it gave the post-Beatles McCartney family a place to live that wasn't swarming with paparazzi. No, the real genius behind moving to the Mull of Kintyre was that its rural tranquility inspired McCartney to write the song of the same name in 1977. It's fair to say that it did well, becoming the UK's biggest ever non-charity single. Note that the bands from the then-new punk rock wave, the music du jour in '77, sounded pretty feeble compared with this song's barrage of bagpipes.

The ultimate supergroup

"Hi, is that Pete Townshend? Paul McCartney here. Yeah, not bad thanks. Listen, I'm putting together a backing band for my new album, *Back to the Egg*. Dave Gilmour of Pink Floyd's doing it, Gary Brooker of Procol Harum is on board, and I reckon I can persuade John Paul Jones and John Bonham of Led Zeppelin to give it a go too. Fancy it?"

Fellow Live Aid performers Pete Townshend and Bob Geldof – along with David Bowie and Alison Moyet (not pictured) – joined McCartney on stage to sing along when his mic failed during *Let It Be*.

"Yep, his mic's definitely on."

It was July 1985, and the biggest live event that has ever been staged was about to end. It was Live Aid, of course, and who better to close the show than the singer from the biggest band ever? Paul took his seat at the piano and began to sing 'Let It Be'. Sources vary as to how many people were watching, from several hundred million to over a billion. What a moment for the microphone to stop working, eh? He soldiered on calmly, a tech fixed it and all was well – but my word, that was a scary moment.

Getty; Alamy (lower right); www.freepik.com

McCartney gives a speech at the Robin Hood Benefit in October 2021. The event raised over $77 million to help lift New Yorkers out of poverty.

Just giving

McCartney has lent his name and support to a whole range of charities. Sure, loads of wealthy celebs do that, you might well say – but few do it with as much commitment as Sir Paul. He has supported Make Poverty History, Adopt-A-Minefield, the Humane Society of the United States, Aid Still Required, Save The Arctic and seal-hunting awareness campaigns among many other causes, as well as appearing on several fundraising records and playing charity shows. Hats off to our man.

Hitting the gas

The film *Spies Like Us*, released in 1985 to widespread apathy, wasn't nearly as good as McCartney's soundtrack, and in particular the song of the same name. What's more, for most of its duration the song itself isn't that great either – until 3'25", that is, when it suddenly doubles in speed and becomes extremely catchy for a bit. That's Macca's arrangement skills for you.

Flowered up

Even the world's most successful songwriter needs a fresh perspective from time to time. However, few such songwriters have the humility to invite a lesser-known talent to collaborate with them, which made it all the more gratifying in 1989 when McCartney's *Flowers in the Dirt* album was released. This LP, a collaboration with the relative whippersnapper Elvis Costello – 35 years old at the time, as opposed to Macca's 47 – was fresh, inspiring and rather good.

Eastern promise

McCartney's 1988 LP *CHOBA B CCCP* – whose title translates as "*Back in the U.S.S.R.*", which Beatles fans will find strangely familiar – was only released in the Soviet Union. Now, that might not sound like a big deal nowadays, but cast your mind back three decades to those dark days for some context. The Soviets were our enemy, the media and governments told us, and allying himself with them – rather than us – was a risky move for McCartney. Of course, the Berlin Wall came down in 1989, *perestroika* ruled the day and the U.S.S.R. vanished almost overnight, so it turned out fine.

ПОЛ МАККАРТНИ

CHOBA B CCCP

Meat is murder

Paul and Linda stopped eating meat in 1975 and soon became animal rights activists, a pursuit which was roundly mocked back in that unenlightened era. As the years have passed and the public has become better educated about climate change, industrialised farming and the health benefits of 'going veggie', it's apparent that the McCartneys were somewhat ahead of the curve. Linda founded an eponymous food company, while Paul regularly supports People for the Ethical Treatment of Animals.

RIGHT: With growing concerns about climate change dominating the news in recent years, Paul's Meat Free Mondays campaign – launched back in 2009 – proved to be ahead of its time.

HEARING ON GLOBAL **AND FOOD POLICY**

Less Meat

EUROPEAN PARLIAMENT
THURSDAY 3 DECEMBER 2009

Less Meat = Less Heat

Paperback writer: At a book signing for *High in the Clouds* in 2005.

"Fans or readers, or even critics, who really want to learn more about my life should read my lyrics."

McCartney introducing *The Lyrics*

Booking ahead

McCartney has become an author in recent years, writing or co-writing two books aimed at kids. The first, *High in the Clouds: An Urban Furry Tail* (2005) concerned a squirrel made homeless by the destruction of its woodland home, and the second, *Hey Grandude!* was created with illustrator Kathryn Durst and published in 2019. While Sir Paul hasn't written a traditional autobiography, in November 2021 he published *The Lyrics: 1956 to the Present* – an intimate self-portrait through his songs.

For fox sake

Fox-hunting has always been a particularly cruel and pointless way to spend your leisure time, but this hasn't stopped certain members of the British public from doing it on a regular basis. What's more, our government is apparently unable either to legislate consistently against this so-called 'sport' or to prevent it from happening. In 2015, McCartney said: "The people of Britain are behind this Tory government on many things, but the vast majority of us will be against them if hunting is reintroduced. It is cruel and unnecessary and will lose them support from ordinary people and animal lovers like myself."

Best buddies

McCartney has worked in film and TV from time to time across his career, as we know, but an especially notable production came in 1985. This was *The Real Buddy Holly Story*, a documentary on the late rock'n'roller – and Macca's childhood idol – which featured a host of notable talking heads. These included Keith Richards, Phil and Don Everly and a host of other famous names. Macca himself occupied a lot of screen time and made his affection for Holly and his music very clear.

ABOVE: Paul and Linda attend a Buddy Holly tribute dinner, with Paul dressed as his idol.

LEFT: Conductor Carl Davis (left) and McCartney at the world premiere of *Liverpool Oratorio* in the Liverpool Anglican Cathedral, June 1991.

Classical gas (part 2)

When you've broken every musical record there is in the rock and pop world, where else is there to go for a real challenge? The answer in McCartney's case was classical music, into whose territory he ventured in 1991 when he composed and recorded with the Royal Liverpool Philharmonic Society. The finished piece, *Liverpool Oratorio*, is a pretty epic work considering that its composer – by his own admission – doesn't even read music.

Paul and Nancy on their wedding day in 2011. They married on 9 October – John Lennon's birthday.

Marrying Nancy Shevell

McCartney was married to Linda for 29 years and then to Heather Mills for a further six, but his third – and one would assume, final – marriage to the American businesswoman Nancy Shevell has made him truly happy, by the looks of things. More similar in demographic and temperament to Macca than her predecessor Mills was, Shevell has that crucial asset when it comes to spouses of famous people – a considerable list of her own achievements. Long may they be happy together.

"You are my rock and roll, you are my A side and B side, you are my verse and chorus."

Paul's message to wife Nancy on the couple's ninth wedding anniversary in 2020

Fuh No One

Fair play to McCartney for refusing to get old gracefully. His 2018 album, *Egypt Station*, featured the song 'Fuh You', which was, quite frankly, about shagging. The news columns frothed with 'Is he too old to sing about sex?' questions, and earnest psychiatrists wrote pieces called 'Sex in old age: let's talk about it'. What a lot of hot air. The subject is fair game for songwriting inspiration for the then 78-year-old musician, just as much as it was for the 27-year-old one back in the day.

Fire Starter!

The producer Martin 'Youth' Glover, once the bassist of Killing Joke, is the other half of The Fireman – McCartney's side project when he's not doing his own material. The music is based on electronica and is by and large pretty interesting stuff, but the point here is not really whether the songs are good or not – it's all about Macca's willingness to step outside the box, ally himself with someone out of his demographic and see what happens. This level of open-mindedness isn't usually seen in rock stars from the Sixties.

RIGHT: When Macca returned to Glastonbury in 2022, he became the oldest headliner in the festival's history.

Glast-Oh Darling

On 26 June 2004, Worthy Farm in Somerset was rocked by the sound of Sir Paul McCartney and his band. Why? Because he was headlining that year's Glastonbury Festival, an absolute masterstroke on the part of organiser Michael Eavis and his family. As for the setlist, where to start? A stack of Beatles classics, a fair dose of Wings, some depth charges for the fans – all of which reminded that year's thousands of attendees that Macca had never gone away. When he returned in 2022, just days after his 80th birthday, the headline performance was hailed as one of the greatest of this generation.

The McCartneys' appearance in *The Simpsons* came with the proviso that Lisa's decision to become a vegetarian was permanent.

Homer run

Forget the millions of album sales and even more millions in the bank, for many successful musicians it's an appearance in animated form on *The Simpsons* that is the real career high point. In 1995, the McCartneys made a guest appearance on an episode called 'Lisa The Vegetarian', with the trademark overbites present and correct. It's pure gold – see it on YouTube without delay.

"

I think people who create and write, it actually does flow – just flows from into their head, into their hand, and they write it down. It's simple...

"

Paul McCartney

Chapter 4
WILD LIFE

COME TOGETHER

Even a knight of the realm needs a network – so let's say hello to the important people in Macca's life

F rom his early years to the present day, there is hardly a relationship in Sir Paul McCartney's life that hasn't been analysed to the point of no return, with endless books, films and documentaries spun off by Beatles experts along the way. And yet it's pretty simple – the man has maintained friendships, family ties and marriages, just as we all do. Who are the people who have sustained Sir Paul through a life well lived?

Childhood friends and family

Friends were important when McCartney was a kid, as they are for all of us. He was always close to his younger brother Mike, and that friendship would have been crucial after the boys' mother Mary died in 1956. Fortunately the McCartneys' extended family was large and supportive, with multiple aunts, uncles and cousins around: in his biography, Paul fondly recalled an Auntie Jin, to whom he was especially close. School friends included Arthur Kelly, who went on to be an actor, and Ivan Vaughan, who introduced McCartney to John Lennon. In addition, there was

Paul dancing with his Aunt Joan after the premiere of *A Hard Day's Night*, July 1964.

Words: Joel McIver. Images: Getty; Mirrorpix via Getty Images (right)

always McCartney's father Jim, a musician who encouraged his sons to play. He supported his son's career and lived until 1976, easily long enough to see the boy become a megastar.

George Harrison

Harrison gets an early mention here because he and McCartney were close friends from a young age, having met in 1954 at Liverpool Institute Grammar School. The year's difference in their ages prevented them becoming truly close until their late teens, but nonetheless the two were a solid unit for life. Although Harrison expressed some mild resentment after The Beatles' split about McCartney's dominance in the band, their friendship endured until the younger man's premature death in 2001. Their collaboration on *The Beatles Anthology* project in 1995 was heartwarming for fans of both musicians.

McCartney later described him as "a lovely guy and a very brave man who had a wonderful sense of humour," adding "We grew up together and we just had so many beautiful times together – that's what I'm going to remember. I'll always love him, he's my baby brother". He played four of his late comrade's songs at the Concert For George in

2002 – 'Something', 'For You Blue', 'All Things Must Pass' and 'While My Guitar Gently Weeps'

Early girlfriends

From the beginning of The Beatles' fame, the four musicians were never short of female attention – especially, as McCartney later recalled, when they lived in Hamburg among strippers and other attentive females. As a teenager he'd had girlfriends called Layla and Julie Arthur, but his major pre-fame relationship was with Dorothy 'Dot' Rhone, who he met in 1959. She travelled to Hamburg with him on one occasion, where he brought her a gold ring, and she became pregnant in 1962. McCartney was prepared to marry her and raise the child; however, she miscarried and the relationship ended soon after. Later, he enjoyed brief relationships with Thelma Pickles, a ex-girlfriend of John Lennon, and Iris Caldwell, the sister of singer Rory Storm.

Jane Asher

The story of McCartney's relationship with the actress Jane Asher is most notable for how he was

exposed to an entirely different world through her relatives. He met her in April 1963 at a Beatles Royal Albert Hall show and moved in with her family soon after. Cultured, sophisticated and embedded in high society, the Asher family – headed by an eccentric doctor and also featuring the singer Peter Asher of the duo Peter and Gordon – gave McCartney entirely new insights into Swinging London. He wrote songs for Peter and Gordon, met writers such as Bertrand Russell and Harold Pinter and wrote Beatles songs including 'Yesterday' at the Ashers' house. The relationship only ended in 1968 when Asher broke off their engagement: McCartney had been unfaithful in her absence.

Linda Eastman

The love of McCartney's life, many observers speculate, must be Linda Eastman, who he met in 1967 and married two years later. He adopted her daughter Heather, and the couple had three more children, Mary, Stella, and James (see below). Linda joined Wings and toured with the band for its entire existence in the Seventies, lending credence to McCartney's later claim that the couple spent only a single week apart throughout

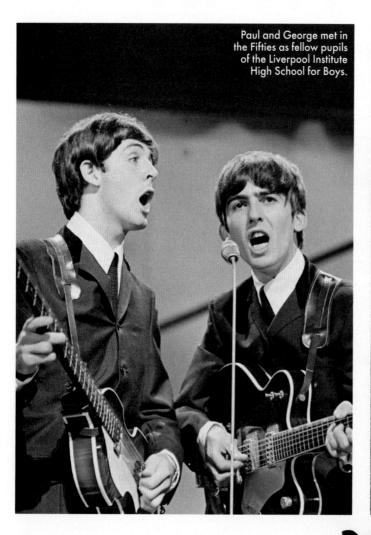

Paul and George met in the Fifties as fellow pupils of the Liverpool Institute High School for Boys.

Paul pictured in December 1967 with then girlfriend Jane Asher and his beloved sheepdog, Martha.

Getty

Before becoming Mrs McCartney, Linda enjoyed a successful career as a photographer. In 1968 she became the first female photographer to shoot a *Rolling Stone* cover.

their 29-year marriage – the week in question being when he was held on drug charges in Japan in 1980. Sadly, Linda died of cancer in 1998, at the age of only 56.

Heather Mills

McCartney was first seen alongside model Heather Mills in 2000. The pair were married two years later and they welcomed a daughter, Beatrice, in 2003. Mills – best known for her work in aid of disability awareness, having herself suffered the loss of a leg, was unpopular with the British press, and the marriage ended in 2008.

Nancy Shevell

Before his divorce with Mills was finalised, McCartney began dating Nancy Shevell in late 2007. She is a businesswoman with various interests, as a member of the board of the New York Metropolitan Transportation Authority and the vice-president of a transportation conglomerate. She and McCartney were married in 2011, the venue being Old Marylebone Town

Paul and Heather first met at the 1999 Pride of Britain Awards.

Paul and Nancy were introduced by the broadcast journalist Barbara Walters, who is Nancy's cousin.

Hall, where he and Linda had been married 42 years before.

John Lennon

It's fair to say that McCartney and John Lennon had a complex relationship. How many bands can last a decade with two lead singers and songwriters fighting for control? Perhaps the two musicians' decision to credit all their songs to 'Lennon-McCartney' helped to keep the relationship serene (although it's notable that McCartney went through a phase of reversing their names in that credit in later life). As we've seen elsewhere, The Quarrymen – and by default The Beatles – started life as Lennon's band, with the older, tougher and more aggressive man the de facto leader. When McCartney started to take control after Brian Epstein's death, it's arguable that the relationship between the two men began to fall apart.

After the band split in 1970, Lennon really let McCartney have it in the form of unpleasant statements in the press. A feud was played out in songs written by both men, although it's likely that this was whipped up by the media into a bigger phenomenon than it really was.

Still, the two musicians socialised on occasion, jamming together in 1974 – released on a bootleg recording, *A Toot and a Snore in '74* – and almost, but not quite, playing in public together two years later. On 24 April 1976, they were watching *Saturday Night Live* at Lennon's home in New York when the host made a $3,000 offer for The Beatles

Paul's friendship with John Lennon was arguably the defining relationship in both of their lives.

The last men standing: Paul and Ringo still perform together occasionally.

to reunite. The two musicians considered calling a cab and going to the nearby studio, but decided against it – supposedly because they were both too tired.

McCartney was crushed by Lennon's murder in 1980, and guested on George Harrison's Lennon tribute, 'All Those Years Ago', the following year. His own tribute song, 'Here Today', was released in 1982.

Sir Ringo Starr

Despite the occasional 'difference of opinion' over The Beatles' career, McCartney and Ringo Starr have enjoyed a reasonably amicable relationship over the last 60 years. There's the famous story of Starr quitting the band a couple of times, of course, and one or two gritted-teeth comments from the drummer such as "Paul is the greatest bass player in the world. But he is also very determined... musical disagreements inevitably arose from time to time." Still, as the rhythm section in The Beatles, the two men would have developed a mutual bond simply through playing in sync together – a tangible benefit of choosing to play bass or drums.

After The Beatles, McCartney and Starr worked together on a frequent basis. The former wrote, sang and played on Starr's 1973 album *Ringo*; Starr acted in McCartney's 1984 film *Give My Regards to Broad Street*, and played drums on the soundtrack album; he played again on McCartney's 1997 album *Flaming Pie*; and they worked together the following year on Starr's *Vertical Man*. Since then, the two musicians have regularly recorded and performed together, and as the last men standing from The Beatles, this is always welcome.

Children

McCartney has five children, beginning with Heather (née See). She was born in Tucson, Arizona on 31 December 1962, and is therefore the only one of his offspring to be born in the pre-Beatlemania world. She is the daughter of the late Linda McCartney and an American geologist called Joseph See Jr., who died in 2000. McCartney married her mother when Heather was six years old and adopted her shortly afterwards. She is a much-travelled printer, photographer and potter, and as well as campaigning for animal rights she

Getty

The McCartney family pose together at the airport in June 1975.

"We were there every night to put them to bed, there in the mornings to wake them up. So even though we were some famous couple, to them we're just Mom and Dad. I think that's what's important... and it worked."

McCartney discussing his and Linda's approach to parenting

James McCartney has followed in his father's footsteps as a musician.

Mary McCartney is a professional photographer, like her mother.

Stella McCartney has forged her own path as a world-renowned fashion designer.

runs a series of household products, the Heather McCartney Houseware Collection.

Paul and Linda's first child together was Mary (born 28 August 1969), who was named after McCartney's mother. She works as a professional photographer and author, having started her career as a photo researcher at the book publisher Omnibus Press. Famous subjects have included former prime minister Tony Blair, Ralph Fiennes and Jude Law, and she manages her mother's archive of pictures at McCartney's company, MPL Communications. Mary is also involved in charitable causes such as Meat Free Monday and Green Monday.

Stella McCartney OBE (born 13 September 1971) is a fashion designer and the best-known of McCartney's children, thanks to the high profile of the industry in which she works. She learned her skills through working for Christian Lacroix and her father's tailor Edward Sexton, and attended Central Saint Martins art college. Many of her garments promote an animal rights message, and she runs stores worldwide, manages a line of skincare products and runs the Stella McCartney Cares Foundation, a charity dedicated to breast cancer research. You may have seen the dress worn by Meghan Markle at her wedding reception; it was a Stella McCartney design.

James McCartney (born 12 September 1977) is a musician who releases his own albums and has played on his father's releases on several occasions. He has yet to make a serious commercial impact, although his statement in 2012 that he was considering forming a 'next generation' version of The Beatles with Sean Lennon, Zak Starkey and Dhani Harrison pricked up a few ears.

Finally, McCartney's youngest child is his daughter Beatrice (born 28 October 2003) from his marriage to Heather Mills.

McCartney also has eight grandchildren – from Mary, Arthur, Elliot, Sam and Sid; and from Stella, Beckett, Bailey, Miller and Reiley. Will we be reading in another 50 years about the prevalence of the McCartney gene in a whole new dynasty of musicians? Watch this space... ⬇

Getty

Family portrait

Paul and Linda were happily married for nearly 30 years, reportedly spending less than a week apart the entire time.

MARCH FOR OUR LIVES 👥👥👥👥

McCartney attending the March for Our Lives protest in New York, March 2018, wearing a shirt reading 'We can end gun violence'.

WE ALL WANT TO CHANGE THE WORLD

From animal rights to peace in the Middle East, Sir Paul McCartney supports a long list of causes

When you're the most popular songwriter on the planet and you'd already earned your first million by the time you turned 23, what keeps you getting out of bed in the morning? In Paul McCartney's case, the certain knowledge that you can use your platform as a recognisable – and popular – figure to make life better for people.

And not just people. Although Macca has been involved in many different charitable causes, the one for which he will always be best known is that of animal rights. The famous story of his awakening to the plight of farmed and slaughtered livestock dates back to 1975, when he witnessed lambs playing in a field while eating a meal of lamb meat, according to *The Beatles Encyclopaedia*, written by McCartney's long-time associate Bill Harry. We've all been in similar situations, but unlike most of us, McCartney and

Paul invested millions in the Linda McCartney brand to ensure their products would remain free from genetically modified ingredients.

Say NO To GMO!

Words: Joel McIver. Images: Getty (left); Alamy/PA Images (right)

his then wife Linda made it their lives' mission to promote better treatment of animals; their children all support the same cause, to a lesser or greater extent.

The context for this has to be understood for the McCartneys' contribution to the animal rights movement to be gauged correctly. In the Seventies, the country was still recovering from the food industry strategies that had kept the population fed since World War II. Battery farming, which we refer to as 'industrialised farming' today, was the norm because it was cheap and efficient, and because getting protein onto the tables of the nation as affordably as possible was a priority. In the days when excess disposable income was an alien concept for most workers, this cheap meat was essential and popular. The idea of an incredibly wealthy celebrity like Paul McCartney telling people not to consume meat at all was at best mystifying and at worst laughable.

For this reason, as well as the fact that meat substitutes weren't as tasty as they are today when this branch of food technology was in its infancy, a lot of people didn't take Linda McCartney Foods seriously when the company was launched in 1991. By then, the idea of treating the planet and its residents more compassionately had entered the mainstream conversation, thanks to the new green movement of the Eighties and related causes such as the anti-nuclear weapons campaign, but the average family was still tucking into industrialised-farmed meat on a daily basis.

Almost 30 years later, vegetarianism, veganism and the climate change protest movement are simply a part of the everyday narrative. Paul and Linda deserve credit for being way, way ahead of

the curve, especially as it hasn't been plain sailing for the LMF company – at one point Macca was obliged to put £3 million into the firm to keep it free of genetically engineered ingredients. In that situation, most companies would have either folded or accepted the unwelcome new additions.

Critics could argue that it's easy to fix a problem when you're in a position to throw millions at it, and they'd be at least partly right – but McCartney consistently puts his mouth where his money is. In 1995, he lent his voiceover skills to a documentary titled *Devour the Earth*, and did the same in 2009 in a video for the People for the Ethical Treatment of Animals (PETA) called *Glass Walls*. He has also allied himself in some way or other with organisations such as the Vegetarian Society, the David Shepherd Wildlife Foundation, Meat Free Monday, the Humane Society of the United States, Humane Society International and World Animal Protection.

McCartney even wrote to the Dalai Lama in 2009, asking him why he ate meat – a remarkably cheeky thing to do, at least on paper. Even more remarkably, he got an answer, with Tenzin Gyatso (as no-one calls him) replying with words to the effect of 'My doctors tell me I must eat meat'. Macca didn't let that slide, explaining "I wrote back again, saying, you know, I don't think that's right... It just doesn't seem right – the Dalai Lama, on the one hand, saying, 'Hey guys, don't harm sentient beings... Oh, and by the way, I'm having a steak." Research reveals that the Buddhist leader eats meat twice a week on medical advice, but that his home is otherwise meat-free and that his teachings do indeed recommend a vegetarian diet. Who would know about any of that without McCartney's involvement?

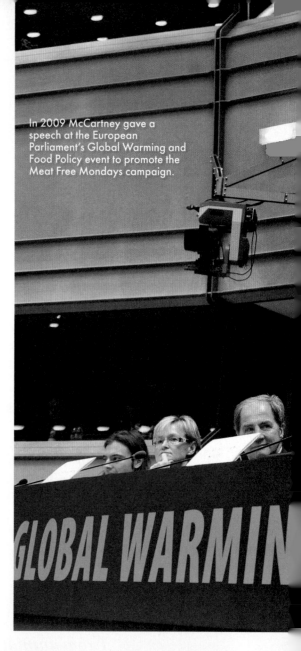
In 2009 McCartney gave a speech at the European Parliament's Global Warming and Food Policy event to promote the Meat Free Mondays campaign.

Paul singing with Bono and the other Live Aid performers during the concert's finale.

AND **FOOD POLICY**

McCartney has even challenged His Holiness the Dalai Lama for eating meat.

"If slaughterhouses had glass walls, everyone would be a vegetarian."

Paul McCartney

On other occasions, McCartney has spoken out about related issues such as seal-hunting – when he took part in a 2006 TV debate on the practice with the president of Newfoundland in Canada – and fox-hunting, which he accurately described in 2015 as "cruel and unnecessary". However, his concerns extend to the human species too: along with Heather Mills, he became a patron in 2003 of Adopt-A-Minefield, encouraging none other than Vladimir Putin to join the campaign at a meeting before a concert in Red Square, Moscow. Did it do any good? Who knows, but that didn't stop McCartney giving it his best shot.

Broader initiatives supported by McCartney over the years have included the Make Poverty History campaign; the US Campaign For Burma, in support of Burmese Nobel Prize winner Aung San Suu Kyi; Aid Still Required, which raised funds in the wake of the Asian tsunami in 2004; Save The Arctic; and the anti-hydraulic fracturing campaign, Artists Against Fracking. Notably, he also supports OneVoice, a movement that attempts to grasp one of the thorniest modern-day issues, the Israeli-Palestinian conflict.

Paul and Linda were flying the flag for vegetarianism decades before it was popular.

This, reads McCartney's website, "appeals to the national self interest of both peoples. They don't ask each side to like or love each other; rather they ask them to recognise the entangled nature of their fates, and the need to address the concerns on each side so that they can fulfil their respective moderate national ambitions."

Musically, of course, McCartney has been a regular participant in charity-affiliated recordings and live events. We've mentioned his role in Live Aid in 1985 and its sequel Live 8 two decades later, as well as his earlier contribution to Ferry Aid's 'Ferry Cross the Mersey'; he also assisted with the Concerts for the People of Kampuchea as far back as 1979. Nowadays he is a supporter of Nordoff-Robbins Music Therapy, which promotes the use of music as a healing tool, and of the Liverpool Institute For Performing Arts (LIPA), described as "a university level institute combining performance, technical innovation, business awareness, understanding and intellectual development". In 2015 he was one of many musicians who contributed to 'Love Song for the Earth', a collaborative project designed to raise awareness of the United Nations Climate Change Conference, held in Paris that year. The song was cheesy, but it educated people, which was the point.

In case you think it's easy to lend your name to causes such as the ones listed above, think again. These organisations require serious amounts of time and energy; they leave you open to ridicule at best, and to a career-threatening controversy at worst; and perhaps most damaging of all, people stop taking you seriously if you campaign a lot. You become known less as a musician than as an earnest, humourless, finger-wagging bore. Don't laugh – it happened to Bob Geldof, it happened to Sting, and it may just happen to Paul McCartney.

Despite all this, our man, approaching 80 and with his time at a premium, still gets deeply involved. We could all learn from his example.

"In case you think it's easy to lend your name to charitable causes, think again. These organisations require serious amounts of time and energy."

Paul and then wife Heather meet a seal pup in the Gulf of St Lawrence, Canada, during a 2006 visit to protest against the controversial annual seal hunt.

Chapter 5
HERE TODAY

LISTEN TO WHAT THE MAN SAID

What's Sir Paul McCartney's legacy? Much more than just the sound of Oasis, that's for sure...

Imagine if you asked Macca to show you his business card in the pub. It would say something like 'Sir Paul McCartney CH, MBE, Academy Award winner (1971), Rock & Roll Hall of Fame inductee (1988, 1999), BRIT Award for Outstanding Contribution to Music (2008), Gershwin Prize (2009), 18 Grammy Awards, Honorary Doctor of Music from Yale University, Honorary Doctor of the University of Sussex, Fellow of the British Academy of Songwriters, Composers and Authors, Légion d'Honneur, Kennedy Center Honors. Available for wedding hire.' That's a big old business card.

If you then asked him 'Oh yeah? What else have you done, Sir Paul?' he would no doubt fix you with an amused glance and say, "Well, if you must know, I have a star on the Hollywood Walk of Fame, I've been nominated as a MusiCares Person of the Year, there is a planet and an asteroid named after me, and I've got over 60 gold discs in the bathroom."

You'd be pushing your luck if you then said, 'Wow. Sold a few records, have you?', but you never know – he might well reply, 'As it happens, yes. I've written or co-written 43 songs that sold over a million copies each. I've charted with 188 different songs. I've had more Number One hits than anyone else in history. Oh, and I wrote a song called 'Yesterday' which has been covered 2,200 times."

Words: Joel McIver. Image: Getty

You might feel a bit stupid and offer to buy him a pint, but then he might say, 'Nah, I'll get 'em in. I've sold 100 million singles and 100 million albums and I'm worth over 1 billion dollars. Tell you what, I'll get you some vegan crisps as well."

And yet these are just the raw numbers. They tell us nothing about McCartney's artistry, or the emotional impact of his songwriting. His personal wealth is certainly a useful barometer of the popularity of his music, but on a global scale, a fortune of 'only' £800m is mundane on a planet where there are over 2,000 living billionaires (thanks, Google). Instead, to gauge his true legacy – which you can interpret as 'success', 'impact', 'brand' or a number of synonyms – we need only to look at the huge number of musicians who have been influenced by his music over the decades. Did we say 'influenced'? In many cases 'ripped off' would be more appropriate...

The Beatles' instantly-recognisable vocal harmonies, image-packed lyrics, earworm choruses, interest in exotic instrumentation – and substances – plus their cheeky look, based largely on haircuts and facial hair, were all being liberally 'borrowed' by their contemporaries when they were barely out of the gate. Look at The Monkees,

for starters. The American Beatles in all but name, there were four of them, they had wacky haircuts by the uptight standards of the day, they sang about girls and cars and had their own TV show. They also had a ton of hits from 1966 onwards. Go figure, as they say.

"What a fucking great band we were."

___

Paul McCartney

A more serious tribute to the Fab Four sound came from The Byrds, a unit of serious creative talent. Roger McGuinn, Gene Clark and David Crosby were initially a folk band until they Beatle-

ised Bob Dylan's 'Mr Tambourine Man' and became massive stars. In fairness to them, Dylan was an equal influence – as indeed he was on The Beatles – and the music fed in all directions, with all three bands taking a keen interest in each other's musical approach.

Then there was The Beach Boys, simple surf-poppers until their leader Brian Wilson heard *Rubber Soul* and created his conceptual masterpiece, *Pet Sounds*, in 1966. "I still remember hearing 'Michelle' for the first time, and 'Girl'. What an incredible song!" he gushed. "The lyrics are so good, and so creative… I can't forget the sitar, too. I'd never heard that before, that unbelievable sound. No-one had heard that in rock'n'roll back then... It really did inspire the instrumentation I ended up using for *Pet Sounds*."

You'll have spotted a common theme here – all these musicians are American. There's a solid reason for this: when The Beatles played *The Ed Sullivan Show* three times in February 1964, the whole nation was transfixed. Various learned observers have commented over the years that the times were right for a bunch of imported musicians to break big in America, at least partly because the country was still reeling from the

The Beatles' first appearances on *The Ed Sullivan Show* in 1964 are arguably the most influential events in music history.

The bronze Beatles sculpture by Andy Edwards was unveiled at Pier Head in Liverpool on 4 December 2015.

murder of President Kennedy just four months previously. True or not, The Beatles influenced an entire generation of music-loving American kids with those TV shows, inspiring many of them into picking up guitars themselves.

For example, Nancy Wilson of Heart once said: "The lightning bolt came out of the heavens and struck [my sister] Ann and me the first time we saw The Beatles on *The Ed Sullivan Show*. There'd been so much anticipation and hype about The Beatles that it was a huge event, like the lunar landing: that was the moment Ann and I heard the call to become rock musicians. They seemed to us then like the punks seemed to the next generation – way out of the box for the time… Right away we started doing air guitar shows in the living room, faking English accents, and studying all the fanzines."

Then there's Billy Joel, who recalled: "The single biggest moment that I can remember being galvanised into wanting to be a musician for life

Nineties Britpop icons Oasis were heavily influenced by The Beatles.

Getty

Sir Paul performing at the Rock and Roll Hall of Fame induction ceremony in 2015. At the 2021 event he inducted Foo Fighters, who have cited The Beatles as one of their influences.

"Now, over 50 years since The Beatles split up, Paul McCartney can hear his influence everywhere."

was seeing The Beatles on *The Ed Sullivan Show*," and whose song 'Scenes from an Italian Restaurant' is a medley of three individual pieces. "It was kind of based on side two of *Abbey Road*," he admitted.

Joe Walsh, guitarist of the James Gang and the Eagles, also said: "I took one look at *The Ed Sullivan Show* and it was, 'Fuck school. This makes it!' I memorised every Beatles song and went to Shea Stadium and screamed right along with all those chicks. My parents still have a picture of me all slicked up, with a collarless Beatles jacket and Beatles boots, playing at the prom." He went further than most Beatles devotees, marrying Marjorie Bach, whose sister Barbara is Ringo Starr's wife.

It didn't stop there, with The Beatles continuing to inspire rock and pop bands long after the group itself parted ways in 1970. Gene Simmons of Kiss, one of the biggest stadium bands of all time, took his cue directly from McCartney. "There is no way I'd be doing what I do now if it wasn't for The Beatles," he said. "I was watching *The Ed Sullivan Show* and I saw them. Those skinny little boys, kind of androgynous, with long hair like girls. It blew me away that these four boys in the middle of nowhere could make that music. Then they spoke and I thought, 'What are they talking like?' We had never heard the Liverpool accent before... They were also a cultural force that made it okay to be different."

From Cheap Trick, the Bee Gees and Pixies, to Bruce Springsteen and The Bangles, there's barely a rock phenomenon who hasn't paid tribute to the Fab Four over the decades. And there's little sign of their influence letting up in the modern era. Sure, Britpoppers Oasis were the best-known emulators of The Beatles sound – as bandleader Noel Gallagher once put it, "It's beyond an obsession. With every song that I write, I compare it to The Beatles" – but it didn't stop there. Dave Grohl of Nirvana and the Foo Fighters said, "When I was young, that's how I learned how to play music – I had a guitar and a Beatles songbook. I would listen to the records and play along... I never had a teacher – I just had these Beatles records."

Now over 50 years since The Beatles split up, Paul McCartney can hear his influence everywhere, in the music of self-confessed disciples such as Paul Weller, Squeeze, Gary Barlow, Crowded House and The Flaming Lips. Even prog-rock and heavy metal has its share of Macca devotees, from Ozzy Osbourne of Black Sabbath to Robert Fripp of King Crimson. In 1999, Fripp wrote: "Were The Beatles the last example of group genius in Western popular culture?" Last example or not, they're certainly the biggest and the longest-lasting – and we're all better off for it. 🎸

President Obama awards Paul with the Gershwin Prize at the White House in 2010. The award celebrates lifetime contributions to popular music.

Getty (left); Yuri Gripas/AFP via Getty Images (right)

Hall of Fame

Paul and Ringo perform together at the latter's induction into the Rock & Roll Hall of Fame in April 2015. Macca himself was inducted in 1999.

THE LONG AND WINDING ROAD

What's been occupying Sir Paul since the year 2000?
A heck of a lot, it turns out – he's still a man on the run

Divide the career of Paul McCartney into decade-long chunks, and you'll notice something rather unexpected. His Sixties were obviously more creatively successful than almost any musician in history, and while his Seventies couldn't quite match that golden decade, he acquitted himself well with Wings and as a solo artist. His Eighties was a decade of two halves, one self-indulgent and one moderately laudable, and in the Nineties he kept the pace, neither increasing nor diminishing his stature in the eyes of the world.

In the 2000s and 2010s, when he should by all reasonable expectations have been slowing down in preparation for retirement, our man has experienced a renewed surge of vitality – and no-one, but no-one, saw it coming. At the time of writing he is in his eighties and still mentally and physically fit, with a command of performance and songwriting that practically none of his contemporaries can hope to equal. On top of that, stadiums full of people still line up to see him play: McCartney's commercial presence in the 2020s is as big as it's ever been. How many other musicians can make the same claim?

Words: Joel McIver. Image: Getty

You could reasonably argue that this renaissance kicked off after the 1995 *Beatles Anthology* project, when McCartney – along with George Harrison and Ringo Starr – finally put the record straight, laying the ghost of John Lennon to rest and casting off the considerable millstone of having been in the biggest band in the world. Free to enjoy his legacy rather than try to outperform it, Macca could then embark on the most prolific period of his career.

This immediately took him in some unexpected directions. In the year 2000, he collaborated on an album of electronica with producer Youth – who had formed the other half of the *ad hoc* Fireman project since 1993 – and the Welsh indie band Super Furry Animals. The album, *Liverpool Sound Collage*, was the obvious next step in a journey that he'd been on since the mid-Sixties, when he first experimented with tape loops and 'musique concrète' in avant-garde London. The songs aren't easy listening by any

> # "Nothing pleases me more than to go into a room and come out with a piece of music."
>
> ---
>
> ## Paul McCartney

means, based on white noise, lo-fi drums and bass and repeated vocal loops, but as Macca himself always thought, the experimental approach matters as much as the results.

More sombre work followed with a choral composition called 'Nova', which also appeared in 2000 on an album called *A Garland for Linda*. This collection of tributes to McCartney's late wife included epic works by luminaries such as John Tavener, but 'Nova' is a high point, based on an emotional soprano ensemble, and rising and falling with considerable dynamic control.

The following year McCartney was engaged in music of similar gravity. On the morning of 11 September 2001, he happened to be on a plane, waiting to take off, at an airport in New York. Looking out of the window, he witnessed the first attack on the World Trade Center, and was asked to leave the plane to seek safety. Over the next few, chaotic weeks he pulled off the remarkable stunt of organising an all-star benefit event, the Concert

McCartney backstage with Kanye West and Rihanna at the Grammy Awards, where they performed 'FourFiveSeconds'.

for New York, which took place at Madison Square Garden on October 20.

The line-up included The Who, James Taylor, Mick Jagger, Keith Richards, Billy Joel, Backstreet Boys, Elton John and other stellar artists, and was rounded off by McCartney himself, whose efforts helped to raise over $35 million for New York's first responders and their families. A decade later a documentary called *The Love We Make* was released; it followed McCartney through those six weeks of frantic activity, and makes a significant addition to the film of the concert itself.

The deaths of Linda (1998) and George Harrison (2001), as well as the shock of 9/11, must have made this period stressful for McCartney, to say the very least. This may explain why Macca flung himself back into his rock'n'roll persona with such vigour, releasing a new, guitars-heavy album called *Driving Rain* in late 2001 and hitting the road.

Accompanied by guitarists Rusty Anderson and Brian Ray, Paul 'Wix' Wickens on keyboards and Abe Laboriel Jr. on drums – a live band which has remained largely unchanged since then – McCartney played all over the planet; the appropriately titled Driving The World Tour grossed $126.2 million, an average of over $2 million per show. The *Back in the World* live album was released in 2003 and signed off McCartney's return to the world stage as a live performer. In truth, he'd never really been away – he'd just had a hell of a lot of life to deal with.

Not that life ever really stops throwing curveballs: McCartney married Heather Mills in 2002, and judging by the details released when the couple divorced six years later, it wasn't always a tranquil union. Still, by this point in his career everything he did was an event, such as two Super Bowl appearances in 2002 and 2005 and an epoch-defining closing appearance at Live 8, also in '05. At the show, held 20 years after the original

Live Aid, he performed 'Sgt Pepper's Lonely Hearts Club Band' with U2, 'Drive My Car' with George Michael, 'Helter Skelter', and 'The Long and Winding Road'.

Not content with heading up these massive events, McCartney was also incredibly busy in the studio. Over a packed four-year period he recorded a rock album, *Chaos and Creation in the Backyard* (2005); a classical work titled *Ecce Cor Meum* ('06); another rocker called *Memory Almost Full* ('07); and another Fireman record, *Electric Arguments* ('08). That's a whole lot of music for a man who had been writing songs professionally for close to 50 years. Consider how many musicians run out of what is referred to in the business as 'creative capital' by their thirties... and then take a look at the McCartney catalogue.

What's more, the rest of his career isn't simply a list of albums and live shows. Read between those details and you'll see a senior musician looking not for inspiration – his alert mind has always supplied him with plenty of that – but for challenges. Take Them Crooked Vultures, for instance – the supergroup comprising Josh Homme of Queens of the Stone Age on guitar, John Paul Jones of Led Zeppelin on bass and the everyman of modern rock, Dave Grohl of Nirvana and the Foo Fighters, on drums.

McCartney told the *Daily Mail* that he was almost recruited to join the band, but Jones got there first. "We went out for a bite to eat and Dave told me he was starting this band with Josh," he said. "I asked him who was playing bass and he rather sheepishly told me he'd approached John. So you read it here first; Paul McCartney was nearly the bass player in Them Crooked Vultures."

Now, did McCartney *need* to join a band? Absolutely not – he was interested simply because the chance to write and record with Grohl and Homme, two of the most creative voices in

Tony Bennett, Lady Gaga, Stevie Wonder and McCartney at Bennett's 90th birthday celebration in 2016.

Getty

Discussing his *Hey Grandude!* book, McCartney said, "I wanted to write it for grandparents everywhere – and the kids – so it gives you something to read to the grandkids at bedtime."

American hard rock, would have been a fascinating opportunity. As it turned out, Them Crooked Vultures divided opinions with the self-titled album they released in 2009, with its total being rather less than the sum of its parts – but it can't be denied that McCartney's presence on it would definitely have made it worth a listen.

The same year our man returned to live touring after four years away from the road. With successful gigs in the USA in particular, it was interesting to note how America has embraced him once more in recent decades. Aware of how pivotal The Beatles were to an entire generation of rock musicians, and with middle-aged record-industry executives nostalgic for the far-off days

when the chirpy moptops appeared in their living-rooms via *The Ed Sullivan Show*, the US music business has provided a willing platform for McCartney right up to the present day. The fact that he now has an American wife undoubtedly helps.

Highlights of Macca's American presence in recent years have included a tribute to *The Ed Sullivan Show* in an episode of *The Late Show With David Letterman* in 2009; three gigs at Citi Field, which replaced the Shea Stadium in Queens, New York, the same year; a double live album called *Good Evening New York City* commemorating those shows; the opening show at the Consol Energy Center in Pittsburgh, Pennsylvania in 2010; and

Paul and Nancy at Buckingham Palace for his investiture in May 2018.

"It gets dangerous when you start believing your own legacy."

Paul McCartney

Macca poses for a selfie with James Corden while filming a Carpool Karaoke special in Liverpool, June 2018.

Getty

McCartney received his star on the Hollywood Walk of Fame in February 2012; The Beatles were given one as a group in 1998.

"McCartney has regularly taken it upon himself to manage The Beatles' legacy."

two sold-out concerts at the new Yankee Stadium in 2011. Do you see Bruce Springsteen, Bob Dylan or any other American artist of McCartney's generation being asked to open British venues on a regular basis? No, you don't, which says something about the ongoing, and welcome, love affair between the USA and The Beatles.

Talking of The Beatles, McCartney has regularly taken it upon himself to manage their legacy. The most striking example of this came in 2003, when at his instigation a revised version of the 1970 swansong album *Let It Be* was released. As you may know, the original LP was produced by Phil Spector – an 'unusual' character and convicted murderer – and contained a large amount of orchestral content which, McCartney felt, detracted from the quality of the songs.

The new version, titled *Let It Be… Naked* as most of Spector's elevator-music slush has been digitally erased, presents the songs in stripped-back form, allowing them to breathe for the first time. In particular, John Lennon's astounding 'Across the Universe' appears in a much simpler, coherent version, as does McCartney's 'The Long and Winding Road'. Spector's original, strings-laden recording of the latter song had irritated Macca so much at the time that he cited it as one

of the reasons why he quit The Beatles – hence his interest in *Let It Be… Naked*, which was a triumph of common sense.

McCartney also helped to promote the video game *The Beatles: Rock Band* in 2009, along with Ringo Starr, Dhani Harrison and George Martin's son Giles. While such games – in which the user 'plays' a song with the aid of an instrument-shaped controller – fell very quickly from fashion a few years later, there's no doubt that this one helped to keep awareness of The Beatles' catalogue high among younger music fans.

Not that McCartney really needs any more fans – it seems that the whole world admires him, from the New York City Ballet, who asked him to compose for them in 2011, to the National

Academy of Recording Arts and Sciences, which named him the MusiCares Person of the Year in 2012. His marriage to Nancy Shevell in 2011 has met with widespread approval, not that the couple needed it – and his appearances at Queen Elizabeth's Diamond Jubilee Concert at Buckingham Palace, and the opening ceremony of the London Summer Olympics, both in 2012, saw him ascend to the very pinnacle of public awareness.

Musically, McCartney remains active on multiple levels. He released an album of covers called *Kisses on the Bottom* in 2012, jammed with three former members of Nirvana at the Concert For Sandy Relief the same year, and released another studio album, *New*, in 2013. Another

Getty

Paul and Ringo pose together at the premiere of *Eight Days a Week* in September 2016.

In 2021, Paul collaborated with Beck on a remix of 'Find My Way', the video for which featured a trippy, 'deepfaked' young Macca.

celebration of *The Ed Sullivan Show* occurred the following year, this time in some depth; McCartney, Starr and others played a 22-song Beatles set in an event called *The Night That Changed America: A Grammy Salute to The Beatles*, with typical showbiz understatement.

He's still exploring new arenas, specifically with a 2014 song called 'Hope for the Future' which closed a video game, *Destiny*, and collaborations with the rapper Kanye West and the singer Rihanna the next year. Although some of the younger fans of the two American artists were slightly confused about who the mature gentleman singing along with their idols actually was, the move was a marketing masterstroke. The same year, Macca sang on a cover of his song

'Come and Get It' by the Hollywood Vampires, a hard rock group featuring Alice Cooper and Johnny Depp – much more familiar territory, and indicative of the fact that our man sees no boundaries when it comes to musical collaboration. He even acted alongside Depp in the blockbuster film *Pirates of the Caribbean: Dead Men Tell No Tales* in 2015 – and why not?

This brings us up to date, with the McCartney brand still very much a cutting-edge concern; his album, *Egypt Station*, went to Number One in America in 2018, for heaven's sake. Even the Coronavirus pandemic didn't slow him down; since 2020, he released his 18th solo album, *McCartney III*; he's working on a stage musical, an adaptation of the 1946 film *It's a Wonderful Life*; he

featured in *McCartney 3, 2, 1*, a documentary miniseries with producer Rick Rubin discussing Macca's entire career; and at the start of November 2021 he released a new book, *The Lyrics: 1956 to the Present* – effectively an autobiography through the prism of his songs. What's more, the long-awaited *The Beatles: Get Back* documentary series from *Lord of the Rings* director Peter Jackson was released in November 2021, and in August 2022 – a week after his 80th birthday – Macca performed a phenomenal near-three-hour headline set at Glastonbury Festival.

We've said it before, but it bears repeating: which musician of Paul McCartney's generation is as creative, as active or as relevant as he is today? There is none; he stands alone. We salute him. ✺

"Why would I retire? Sit at home and watch TV? No thanks. I'd rather be out playing."

Paul McCartney

On stage at Glastonbury 2022 with special guests Dave Grohl and Bruce Springsteen.

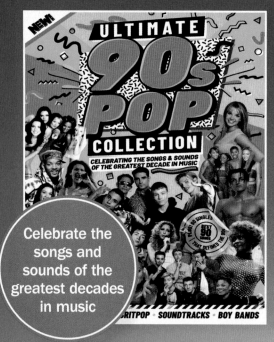

Celebrate the songs and sounds of the greatest decades in music

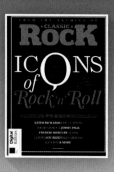

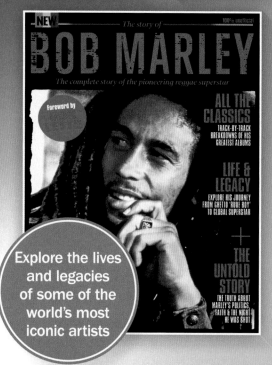

Explore the lives and legacies of some of the world's most iconic artists

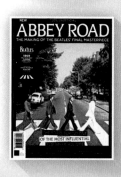

Crank up the volume and get to know the best rock and metal bands on the planet

Get great savings when you buy direct from us

1000s of great titles, many not available anywhere else

World-wide delivery and super-safe ordering

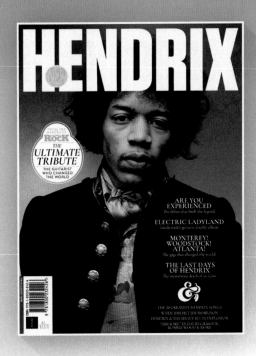

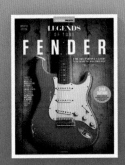

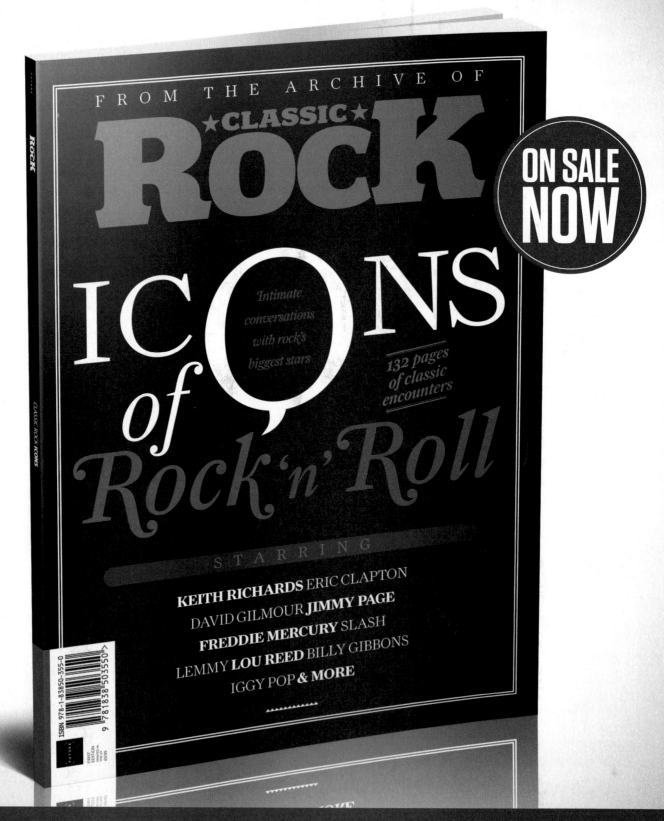